LILY'S HOMECOMING UNDER FIRE

Calla Lily Mystery #1

Anna Celeste Burke

Books by USA Today and Wall Street Journal Bestselling Author Anna Celeste Burke

Murder at Sea of Passenger X Georgie Shaw Cozy
 Mystery #5
Murder of the Maestro Georgie Shaw Cozy Mystery #6
A Tango Before Dying Georgie Shaw Cozy Mystery #7
A Canary in the Canal Georgie Shaw Cozy Mystery #8
 [2019]

A Body on Fitzgerald's Bluff Seaview Cottages Cozy
 Mystery #1
The Murder of Shakespeare's Ghost Seaview Cottages
 Cozy Mystery #2
Grave Expectations on Dickens' Dune Seaview
Cottages Cozy Mystery #3
A Fairway to Arms in Hemingway Hills Seaview Cottages
Cozy Mystery #4 [2019]

Lily's Homecoming Under Fire Calla Lily Mystery #1
A Tangle in the Vines Calla Lily Mystery #2
Fall's Killer Vintage Calla Lily Mystery #3 [2019]

Dedication

To the love of my life who's made
every day an adventure,
under fire or not!

Table of Contents

Acknowledgements

Thanks to my husband, who listened as I read *Lily's Homecoming Under Fire* aloud—more than once! His patience, feedback, and support are always welcome—especially when I feel bogged down.

Thanks as well to Peggy Hyndman, who was the first editor on the manuscript before it was included in the Love Under Fire box set, and who edited again for this standalone version. I'm always grateful for her attention to detail and valuable feedback about content and grammar. Not to mention, she works with amazing grace "under fire" when up against a deadline!

I'm also grateful to Ying Cooper who is a second editor on this book. Her sharp eyes and checks regarding my use of names and places are invaluable, in addition to hunting down typos and skipped words. No author could possibly be more blessed than I am to have such a capable woman working with me. Thank you, Ying!

Andra Weis also provided wonderful feedback as an early reader and identified several awkward passages that I hope I've made easier to read in this version. The encouraging feedback from readers of advanced copies of this first book in the Calla Lily Mystery series have me relishing the prospect of writing more mysteries about Lily, Austin, Judy, Jesse, and all the interesting women in Lily's "diva posse."

1

Coming Home

THE FIRST BULLET whizzed by my head. I saw a flash of light but couldn't make sense of what was happening even when the bullet found a target behind me. I stood, frozen in place, on the front porch of the elegant private cottage Aunt Lettie's lawyer had reserved for me. I hugged Marlowe who was barking fiercely and took a step backward into the foyer. Marlowe wriggled free and jumped to the floor.

A hand holding a white Stetson whacked the porch light, shattering the fixture and the bulb. The owner of the Stetson bumped into me as he bounded indoors. That sent me sliding over the polished wood floor of my rustic chic suite. I yelped as I landed on my well-padded derriere and a barrage of bullets flew over my head.

My heart raced as the shots sank into some surfaces and ricocheted off others. When I struggled to sit up, the stranger tackled me and forced me flat onto the floor. I fought to wrestle free. Marlowe snarled and pulled furiously at the man's sleeve.

"Stay down," he said as he rolled off me. He shook his

arm forcefully, and Marlowe tumbled away, end over end. Furious, I punched the man as he kicked the door shut with a firmly planted, exquisitely carved leather boot. In almost the same motion, he reached up and yanked the lamp off a table near the entry. As the room went dark, two bullets slammed into the heavy wooden front door and sent splinters flying.

Moonlight streamed in through the sliding doors leading outside from the great room behind me. As my eyes adjusted to the darkness, I could see the shadowy figure straining to shove the sofa in front of the door. Marlowe had a grip on his pant leg, growling and shaking his head as he tore at the fabric.

Were Marlowe and I being taken as hostages? I wondered as my stomach roiled in terror.

As my would-be captor peeked through the blinds he'd shut, I flipped over onto my belly and scrambled, crablike, toward the safety of my master suite. The door could be bolted from inside. I didn't get far before he grabbed me and pressed me flat again, knocking the wind out of me. The bullets shattered glass, and the maniac returned fire shooting at someone behind us. My heart sank as I realized he had a gun.

In the distance, I could hear a siren blaring. As it drew closer, I heard shouts, and then footsteps. The footsteps came from the deck outside my bedroom. A minute or two later, tires screeched as a vehicle took off.

"I've told you, already—stay down." This time when he rolled away, the intruder pulled a phone from a pocket. Then he handed Marlowe to me. "Take this and keep it quiet."

"Rikki," he said almost immediately after he placed a call. "I've got a situation on my hands." Those sirens blared now. I imagined them racing toward us up the long driveway leading from the roadway to the cottage.

I considered making a run for it again while the madman spoke on the phone in a low voice. The sofa blocked the front door, but maybe I could escape out the sliding doors to the deck and take the same route the gunman had used. With my luck, running in the dark, I'd impale myself on an enormous shard of glass. A piece of glass might make a good weapon, though. With my free hand, I carefully explored the floor around me, searching for anything that I could use to hurt this guy. He hadn't even flinched when I landed a blow earlier.

"How should I know? Give me a second and I'll ask her." No longer speaking in a whisper, his voice jolted me.

"My boss has a question for you." The glow of light from his phone lit the space around him. He was leaning back on his haunches, squatting down like a catcher behind home plate. "Who wants you dead?"

"Me?" I replied. "Why would anyone want me dead? Those psychopaths must have been after you! Why did you lead them here? Ask 'your boss' who's going to pay for the destruction they left behind? Not me, I can assure you." I was growing angrier by the minute.

"She has no idea," he said to the person on the other end of that call. "Okay, thanks." He slipped the phone into a shirt pocket. Then he held out a hand.

"I'm Deputy U.S. Marshal Austin Jennings."

"Lily Callahan," I replied.

"Lily, I'm glad to meet you, although I wish we were

saying hello under better circumstances. You're safe. The bad guys are gone, and the cavalry will arrive any minute now. May I help you up?" The sirens wailed, hurtling toward us.

"Yes, if you promise not to tackle me again." I took his hand, and he pulled me to my feet. "Shoot!" I exclaimed as I stood. During the fracas, I must have busted a heel on my favorite pair of ankle boots. The pricey designer boots had been one of the gifts in a swag bag at the Emmy Awards ceremony I'd attended a couple of years ago.

"Are you okay?" Austin asked as I lost my balance and fell forward, right into his arms. My head rested on his chest for a split second. I could hear his heart pounding. The scent of the outdoors clung to him despite the fact he was damp with sweat from exertion. His embrace was comforting, although I still had the urge to wring his neck. In part, he'd worked up that sweat by wrestling me to the floor more than once. I held onto his arm as I reached down, unzipped the boot, and removed it.

"Ooh, ouch!" I said as I did that. "Don't worry. I'm sore, but nothing's broken except the heel on my boot." When I looked up, he'd bent over a little to see what I was doing. His face, cast in moonlight and shadow, was closer than I'd expected, and my lips brushed against his cheek when I spoke. "Sorry," I said as I put my unclad foot back onto the floor, still a little wobbly.

"Hang on," he said. "I'm going to take off the other one for you." He smiled for the first time. I couldn't help returning his smile, even though I still held him accountable for one of the most terrifying events of my life.

Apparently, Marlowe had completely forgiven him. He stood next to Austin with his tail whipping the marshal's arm near where my pint-sized pooch had previously tried to sink his teeth into it. Out in front of my guest house, I could hear vehicles screeching to a halt and doors slamming. I'm not sure why Marlowe wasn't concerned about the disturbance going on outside.

There's still a disturbance going on in here, too, I thought. I sucked in a tiny gulp of air when Austin gently, but firmly, grasped my calf, and lifted my foot. I clutched his shoulder to steady myself. He unzipped the boot, and then slowly removed it before placing my foot back onto the floor.

"That's better isn't it?" He asked as I let go and he stood up not more than a few inches from me. So close, I could feel the warmth radiating from his body. I nodded. I wasn't sure if he could see my response in the pool of moonlight that was still the only source of illumination in the room.

"Thanks," I whispered, managing just that one word before Marlowe's tail stopped wagging. What sounded like a platoon of soldiers stormed up the porch steps. It wasn't until someone pounded on the door that Marlowe began to bark again.

"Austin, Rikki just called. Will you let us in and tell us what the hell is going on?"

"Give me a minute," Austin hollered. He dashed to the door and moved the sofa out of the way. The door swung open, and flashlights sought us out. The beams moved from Austin to me. They lingered there until Marlowe growled and they put him in the spotlight.

A uniformed officer I guessed to be in his early fifties was the first person over the threshold. Before I could get a good look at him, he flipped a wall switch, and I had to shield my eyes when the overhead lights came on. They were way too bright after what I'd experienced as an eternity of moonlight and madness.

"Holy crap!" Another officer cried as he stepped through the doorway and scanned the carnage. The extent of the damage was stunning.

"Marlowe! Come!" I commanded. My obedient Miniature Pinscher sprang into my arms as more people filed into the room. I felt exposed standing there barefoot and disheveled. Or, maybe it was because Austin Jennings hadn't taken his eyes off me since the lights went on.

"Oh, no! This is a disaster," a man said. Wearing a sports coat emblazoned with the resort logo, he had to be the resort's night manager. "I demand you answer Sheriff Conner's question, Marshal Jennings."

"Lily Callahan is that you?" A younger officer asked. "It's me, Denny Saunders. I haven't seen you in years except on TV. What are you doing here?"

"I've come home."

"What a homecoming, huh? You sure know how to make an entrance! This is like something out of a movie—Lily's Homecoming Under Fire!" He grinned from ear to ear, gesturing as though he was reading the title on a theater marquee. "Welcome home."

2

The Morning After

I STUMBLED OUT of bed the next morning, disoriented when I awoke to someone pounding on my door. I knew Marlowe wasn't any happier than I was about it by the way he was snarling and barking. When the events from last night suddenly rushed in on me, I went on alert.

"Marlowe!" I called in a hushed tone. "Come!"

I slipped on the soft chenille robe the resort provides to guests even in their more modest accommodations. The resort manager finally got over his huffy tone about the disaster in my cottage when I threatened to sue him because of the lousy security. He'd blanched when I asked him to consider what it could mean if word got out that two well-armed men had managed to get into the resort, destroy one of their pricey, exclusive properties, and nearly kill the occupant.

"Maybe it's our luggage," I muttered as I hurried to the door. "I bet you'd like your breakfast, wouldn't you?" Marlowe wagged his tail. His food and dishes, like everything else I'd taken into the cottage, had been left behind last night. Fortunately, I hadn't unpacked much—

figuring that in a night or two I'd be in my own bed at Aunt Lettie's house.

The police asked me to leave without collecting much more than my purse and a pair of shoes. I flushed remembering how the marshal had helped me slip out of my boots. *What is my problem?* I wondered. I couldn't remember ever having met a man who'd managed to get under my skin as quickly as Austin Jennings had.

"It's a strange bonding thing, I bet, Marlowe." Marlowe made this funny little chuffing sound that I took to mean he agreed with me.

I hoped someone with the resort had brought my car, too. I'd left it parked in the cottage garage while police investigators searched the property for shells and other evidence about the shooters. Who knows what condition the car or my other possessions were in. When I peeked through the peephole, my mouth fell open.

"What do you want?" I asked when I'd opened the door as far as I could without undoing the chain.

"I've got your luggage—and a few questions—for you." Austin stood there with my bags next to him and a basket in his hands.

"Should I put on body armor under my robe first?" I didn't wait for a reply. I shut the door, gave the belt on my robe a tug, and then opened the door wide. "What's that?"

"Breakfast!" Austin announced as he zipped past me into the hotel room and set the basket on a small dining table just off the kitchenette.

My new suite was nice, but nothing like the cottage Franklin Everett had reserved for me. The manager claimed this was the best he could do under the circumstances. I hadn't raised a fuss. After being hunted like a deer, the cottage in the woods had lost its charm. The adrenalin that had raged through my body during the onslaught gave way to exhaustion as I let the resort manager drive Marlowe and me to the hotel.

"For you, too, Marlowe!" Austin tossed a little bone-shaped dog biscuit that Marlowe caught in the air. "His bowls and dog food are in the paper sack along with a few other personal items you left in the master bath."

I stepped into the hallway and grabbed the bag. I snagged the handle on a big roller bag too and dragged it into the room. Austin was out there in a flash and hauled in the rest of my luggage.

"I brought in everything from your car since I wasn't sure what you needed for today. Somehow, the garage and your car were undamaged. Want me to set up breakfast on the balcony?"

"Won't I make myself an easy target for whoever you believe is trying to kill me?"

"Unless the next person who comes after you is a hotel guest or an employee, you'll probably live through breakfast."

"What about the storm troopers who were following you around last night?"

"They weren't following me. I was following them. I had them cornered, too, when I saw one of them aim at you. If I hadn't thrown him off at the last second, that first bullet wouldn't have missed. You can tell they weren't happy about it by what happened after that. Guns for hire don't get full payment until the target is delivered." An image of myself strapped to the top of a truck with a bullet in my head flitted through my mind.

"Let's stay inside." Compared to SoCal, it's nippy out there for summer, but it wasn't the weather that sent a chill through me. I poured kibble into a bowl for Marlowe and filled another bowl with water. When I bent over, I was rewarded with a sharp pain that skittered up my spine. Probably a casualty of one of the wrestling matches I'd had with the marshal. I sat down on the sofa in the small sitting area in my suite. "Over here, okay? I'm too sore to sit in one of those wooden chairs."

Austin nodded as he opened the basket and pulled out a thermal pot of coffee. He found two large mugs in a cupboard above the sink and filled them. The aroma sliced like a knife through the fog in my head.

"Black?" Austin asked, holding out a mug.

"I'll take it any way I can get it," I replied, reaching for the steamy brew. He smirked and raised an eyebrow. "Oh, come on, how old are you? Twelve?"

"Sometimes our subconscious mind takes advantage of us in an unguarded moment." The smirk spread into a wide grin that was hard to resist. I shook my head, and then returned the smile.

"In your dreams," I murmured as I sipped my coffee.

How old is he really? I wondered. Thirtyish was my best guess. There were a few of the tell-tale lines that come with age around his brown eyes that were flecked with gold. Who knows how time affects a man who routinely deals with incidents like the one I survived last night.

Austin caught me scanning his face and smiled. That made the gold flecks in his eyes dance. He took a swig of his coffee and then set it down on the table in front of me. The table looked like three polished tree stumps that had been shoved together. After living in Hollywood for more than a decade, I'd forgotten how much they love wood in all its knotty glory around here.

Austin sauntered back to the table and pulled more items from the basket—muffins, fruit, and ham so smoky I could smell it from here. He'd set his Stetson on a table near the door when he came into the room. Once he'd dropped the rest of my luggage and locked the door, he'd also taken off a fleece-lined suede bomber jacket and hung it on a nearby hook. The hunter green t-shirt he wore underneath the jacket clung to his body. I tried not to stare at it or his well-fitting jeans as he stood at the kitchen table.

"Where's your star, Marshal?"

"I'm not on duty. I arrested the bad guys, so I get a day off."

"You did? I heard them take off, didn't I?"

"Yes, but I knew where they were going—a cabin not far from where they went after you. I would have arrested them earlier, but I wanted to find out what they were doing. They were way too busy for a couple of guys just here to kick back and tour the wineries. Besides, one of them is a wanted fugitive which is why I tracked him here in the first place." He sat down next to me and handed me a plate of food.

"So, what does any of this have to do with me?"

"The fugitive I picked up is wanted for murder. Not one, but several. All of them carried out quietly and professionally without the hitch he ran into last night."

"How is it possible that a guy like that is running around free?"

"He's a pro. No one even knew who he was until law enforcement picked him up in Texas on a speeding violation. They found an unregistered firearm in his car, took him into custody, and charged him with a minor offense. He skipped out before his court appearance. When they ran the gun through ballistics, they got a match to a couple of unsolved shootings. The name he gave to the police was a fake, but they had a mug shot and his prints. The FBI was hunting for someone who fit his description, and that turned his arrest warrant issued in Texas into a national problem for him. Long story short, the U.S. Marshal Service was assigned to bring him in when his prints turned up in the Bay Area on the body of a woman. The husband caved when the police questioned him and admitted he'd hired Aldon Kutchner to kill his wife."

"This is fascinating, I admit," I said as I tore off a tiny bite of ham for Marlowe who was begging in a polite way. He could beg all he wanted and wouldn't get any more. The ham was delicious, and I was ravenous. "I don't have a husband. Never have. I can't think of anyone in real life I've ticked off enough to put out a hit on me. My character died that way, but I can't believe a crazed fan would have the kind of money it would take to hire a pro. I got plenty of hate mail over the years from people who confused my character with me, but no one ever came after me."

"Someone decided to kill off your character in *Not Another Day*."

"Don't tell me you're a soap fan?"

"No, but after last night my boss, Rikki Havens, ran a background check on you. She sent me the report this morning. Who decided to have a hitman kill the Andra Weis character you played for years?"

"I don't know. I figured it was a publicity stunt or they wanted to bring in a younger vixen to cause trouble. Maybe my agent pushed too hard to get me more money when my contract came up for renewal, and they bumped me off rather than give me a raise. To be honest, I was sick of the role and hopeful I could land something else." I sighed. "That didn't happen, so here I am."

"Was your agent okay with your plan to leave Hollywood?"

"How personal is the information in that report?" I asked.

"You're a public figure and so is your agent. The breakup wasn't long ago, and it got plenty of media play. The husband I mentioned who put out the hit on his wife did it because she asked for a divorce. Some men don't handle rejection well."

"Tony and I were done long before we made it official. That I couldn't get him to be straightforward about what happened to my character in *Not Another Day* was part of a bigger problem in our relationship. Agents hustle the truth all the time. I got tired of being hustled. Tony Allen can handle rejection—it's in the job description for Hollywood agents. Besides, it wasn't more than a couple of weeks before he was seen out on the town with Paramount Pictures latest 'it girl,' Elle Keenan. Fast work unless he was already wooing her before we called it quits.

Wasn't his new conquest in the report your boss dug up overnight?" I stabbed a bite of cantaloupe on my plate and shoved it into my mouth.

"It sounds like it's been a rough year," Austin said. When I glanced at him, he was peering at me the way he had last night. I squirmed a little under his scrutiny. I must look like hell since I hadn't put on makeup or done my hair. Then he shook his head and spoke again.

"If you don't mind my saying so, Tony Allen's a damn fool. Elle Keenan may be younger, but I heard her do an interview and she couldn't put two words together without giggling or saying something ridiculous. Too plastic, too. There wasn't anything natural about her." Austin reached over and tucked a loose curl behind my ear. "Want more coffee?"

"Please. More ham, too, if there's any left." All I need is to pile on a few more pounds, but what the heck. I wasn't going to be standing in front of a camera that adds ten pounds, so I have a little leeway.

"More ham and coffee coming right up!" Austin beamed another of those amazing smiles, and I felt myself relax. He exuded confidence—even moved in a way that somehow made me feel everything was going to turn out all right.

"If Tony Allen's upset with me at all, it's not about the end of our affair, it's because I canned him as my agent. I'm not the first one of his clients to dump him. In fact, he's had almost as bad a year as me."

"I'll ask Rikki's investigators to check him out a little more. If he blames you for the bad year he's had, revenge could be a motive. He hasn't taken out any life insurance on you, has he?"

"The studio, yes, but not Tony—at least as far as I know." I tried to remember if I'd ever signed anything he put in front of me without reading it thoroughly. No. I never trusted him that much even when I was his "it girl."

"I'm glad you caught up with those maniacs who shot at me. Can't you rough them up, and get them to tell you who hired them? What if they have me mixed up with someone else?"

"Roughing them up will only give their lawyers wiggle room to get the charges against them dismissed based on a procedural error or a violation of their rights. I don't want to give them that option. 'Lawyer' was the first word out of their mouths, so we'll do what we can, but we won't get much."

"Can't you get one of them to rat out the other one?"

"The authorities will try, but these rats may be more scared of each other than they are of going to prison. The fact that a member of law enforcement was tailing them and witnessed their attempt to kill you might make a deal more appealing. Even when things move without a hitch in the criminal justice system, it takes time." Austin handed me more coffee and then sat down and divided the remaining ham between us. "Time's not on our side until we figure this out. I don't believe this was a case of mistaken identity, Lily. Nor do I believe it's over." I gulped when I saw the darkness enter his eyes as if he was looking inward—was it into his past or my future?

"It would be foolish to try again, wouldn't it?"

"It's a given that whoever's behind hiring someone to kill you is a fool. Whatever problem you pose for someone—a problem that person believes murder will solve—hasn't gone away. I know you told your old friend last night that you've come home. Why?"

3

Aunt Lettie's Legacy

"MY AUNT, LETITIA Morgan, died, and left me her home. It's where I grew up once my parents decided I'd inherited too many of the 'black sheep' genes from the Bankhead branch of the family. That's Bankhead as in Hollywood actress, Tallulah Bankhead. She mortified her fine, upstanding old Alabama family by going to Hollywood back in the day. I'd just turned twelve when my mother and her new husband, Edward Callahan, shipped me out west."

"I'll bet you were a handful even at twelve." The twinkle had returned to Austin's eyes, and that tantalizing grin was on his lips again, too. He was sitting a little closer to me now, or maybe I'd just become more aware of his presence. When I reached for my plate, his hand brushed mine, sending a little charge through me. I responded to his comment before I lost my train of thought.

"I was a miserable little bitch, I confess. I didn't like Callahan or the idea that my mother had become involved with another man so soon after she and my father divorced. He made it clear that adopting me soon after he married my mother was a grand gesture. Changing my name didn't make me feel any better. If anything, it further alienated my father who was already done with us, or so it seemed. I couldn't understand most of what was going on around me, but I was miserable and did my best to make everyone pay. I ditched school and mouthed off when I did go to class. They suspended me. I ran away, and the police found me sitting at a bus station on my way to my dad's house. Not that he'd invited me there." I shrugged.

"That only went on for a few months before I'd 'embarrassed them for the last time,' as my parents put it and called Aunt Lettie. My mother was pregnant at the time, so she probably didn't feel like wrestling with me. Still, I don't believe my acting out brought more shame on my parents than they did. At the time, I didn't get what it meant when my half-sister was born as a 'preemie'—six months into their marriage. A nine-pound preemie Aunt Lettie told me years later when I was wondering for the zillionth time what I'd done to warrant rejection."

"You don't have to explain family dysfunction to me. I lived on and off with grandparents while my parents tried to make up their minds about whether they wanted to be married or not. I guess we're both lucky we had someone willing to play back-up for our parents' screw ups."

"You're fortunate to be so clear that it was their screw up and not yours."

"I didn't have anyone telling me I was destined to become a black sheep if that's what you mean, but kids always find a reason to blame themselves. My parents made it obvious to everyone we knew that their relationship was a problem. It sounds like yours tried harder to keep their marital problems behind closed doors. That was probably easier to do once they got rid of a mouthy twelve-year-old who might have wondered out loud about a nine-pound preemie if she'd been there when the baby was born."

"Well, they weren't in any hurry for me to return. Maybe I was a reminder to Mom and her new husband that their happy home was built on a less than solid foundation. In any case, Aunt Lettie was wonderful. I felt loved, and I appreciated her nonjudgmental, free-spirited approach to life. She wasn't quite like Auntie Mame in the movie, but I did have an interesting, unconventional life. I'll miss her." I sipped my coffee, lost for a moment in the sorrow about Aunt Lettie's passing. Dodging bullets had interrupted my grieving. "I was shocked that she died so suddenly."

"Was there anything dodgy about her death?" Austin asked as he shoved things around on the tree stump coffee table to put up his long legs. Marlowe took that as an invitation to have a seat on his lap. Austin patted Marlowe's little head, and then looked at me waiting for me to answer his question.

"Not according to her lawyer. Franklin Everett says she had a heart condition and died from a heart attack. I didn't get back here often, given my filming schedule, but Aunt Lettie paid me regular visits. When I saw her a few weeks ago, she seemed to be her usual boundless bundle of energy. I was down about the sudden change in my circumstances, although I didn't tell her how bad things were." My eyes flicked toward Austin as I confessed yet another embarrassing fact about myself. He nodded as though he understood. "Maybe she sensed it, or maybe she was sicker than she let on. She suggested I return home and try my hand in local and regional theater. There are plenty of opportunities in wine country and the Bay Area to perform live."

"Why didn't you do it?"

"I hadn't hit rock bottom yet, and it felt too much like giving up. I don't know, maybe like I was being sent packing to Aunt Lettie again. Here I am, now—about to take possession of Lettie's house and the acre or so it sits on. I don't know what else she left me in her Will. A consortium runs the Calla Lily Vineyards and Winery, so I don't know what that means for me. I presume that'll all be clear after the reading of the Will today."

"Do me a favor, okay?" I raised an eyebrow, wondering what Austin had in mind.

"I will if I can, sure." I searched his face waiting to hear what he had to say.

"Ask your aunt's lawyer what happens to your inheritance if someone kills you."

"You don't mince words, do you?"

"I'm trying to get through to you. If no one in Hollywood is angry with you, then you need to consider another possibility. Not everyone may be as eager as Officer Denny Saunders was last night to welcome you home."

"That's as ridiculous as the idea that Tony Allen hired someone to bump me off. Aunt Lettie made sure I didn't get into the kind of trouble here that I caused in Montgomery. I don't even remember giving anyone a hard time. I made friends right away. That's one reason I decided to stay here even when my parents made a couple of superficial gestures at reconciliation."

"Which is why I want you to find out who else stands to inherit Aunt Lettie's property if you're out of the picture. Given the value of property in this area, you're inheriting much more than a few black sheep genes—if such a thing even exists. The house and land alone must be worth millions, Lily. If she also left you a share in the vineyards and winery, you've just become a very wealthy woman. Money is right up there with revenge and love gone wrong as a motive for murder."

"I wasn't involved in the business side of things, but I heard Aunt Lettie talking about it all the time. It's a tough business, so I never thought of Aunt Lettie as rich. I loved the vineyards growing up. They're magical. Aunt Lettie and I wandered through them, taking in the gorgeous views of the countryside. We'd take a picnic lunch out there. My friends and I would put on shows for Aunt Lettie and her friends. It's hard to describe how enchanting I found the vines beautifully spaced in symmetrical rows, with their grapes hanging in luscious bunches. I suppose that's why she changed the name soon after I arrived. Calla Lily—the flower—is a nickname Aunt Lettie gave me. It's short for Lillian Callahan." I teared up recalling those wonderful sunny days with Aunt Lettie.

"I can't believe she's dead and someone's trying to kill me. What am I going to do?" It all suddenly seemed to be too much, and a sob escaped despite my best efforts to choke it back.

Austin reached out, grabbed my hand, and pulled me toward him. I leaned sideways and put my head on his shoulder as he slid an arm around me. Marlowe climbed into my lap and got as close to my face as he could. As if trying to figure out what was wrong and fix it, the sweet little guy put his paws on my shoulders, looked me in the eye, and gave me a nudge with his tiny nose. I pulled him close and gave him a smooch which set his tail wagging. With a woof, he bounded from my lap. After a romp and a roll, he was back and so delighted that I couldn't help smiling.

"This isn't easy, I know. I'm sorry this is happening to you. Let's find out what's going on, okay? I'll try to choose my words more carefully."

"I don't think there's a nice way to say someone wants me dead. If he doesn't bring it up at the reading of the Will this afternoon, I'll ask Franklin Everett who gets what in the event of my untimely death." That got my blood boiling. Anger has always worked for me as an antidote to self-pity and loss. "I suppose I should ask him about having an autopsy done on my aunt, too, before she's laid to rest. When he called me in LA, we settled on a time to meet, and Franklin said he'd make a reservation at the resort. I was so shaken by his call, that I didn't even ask who'd discovered Aunt Lettie's body. There must be a report detailing the circumstances surrounding her death, right?" I sat up straight and wriggled free of Austin's arm, although I held onto his hand for a few seconds longer as I placed it on the sofa between us.

"I can ask. If there is one, Supervisory Deputy U.S. Marshal Rikki Havens ought to be able to get it as part of an ongoing investigation into the attempt on your life. At the very least, it ought to give us a lead about when the locals knew your aunt died and that you were likely to be returning to the area soon. I can tell you that the two men who went after you last night didn't follow you from LA. That means they not only knew you were coming home, but when you were returning and where you were staying. How well do you know Attorney Everett?"

"Not well at all. Until a few years ago, one of Aunt Lettie's oldest friends was her attorney. Chuck Hampton wasn't nearly as articulate as Franklin Everett, with whom I've only spoken once, but he was sharp, and I never doubted he had Aunt Lettie's best interests at heart. He set up the reservation for me at the resort. He or someone who works for him must have let the information get out."

"I don't mean for you to jump to conclusions. Lots of people could have spread the word that Lily Callahan, the hometown girl with a lead role in *Not Another Day*, was coming home for her aunt's funeral. A star-struck employee at the resort could have shared the information. I wouldn't put it past members of the resort management to drop your name as a guest given your celebrity status."

"I hear you. I'll try to keep an open mind about Franklin Everett. He was kind enough when he called to tell me about Aunt Lettie's death and the fact that I was named in her Will to inherit the home where I grew up and other assets." I shrugged. "Even if he decided to hire a hit man to kill me for some reason, what choice do I have but to play this out?"

"What time is your meeting with him?"

"This morning at eleven in his office in Calistoga, not too far from Aunt Lettie's house and the vineyards. He's supposed to give me the keys, the deed, and whatever else I need to take possession of the house. He seemed to believe I could stay there tonight if I wanted to."

"Why don't you call me when you're finished with the lawyer, and I'll meet you at the house to check it out? It wouldn't hurt to spend another night or two here before you move in there alone."

"I can stay here again tonight, but I should probably get settled in at the house tomorrow. I have movers bringing my stuff from the condo the next day. Who knows when they'll show up or where I'll put it all when they do. Besides, I won't be completely alone. There's a foreman and a crew who tend to the vineyards. The foreman has a caretaker's cottage down closer to the road where the gates are. There's a bunkhouse on the property for the crew. The bunkhouse doesn't always get much use, but since Jesse's gearing up for the harvest season that will start in a few weeks, it's occupied right now."

"Let me check in with Rikki and see what she can find out about your Aunt Lettie's death. If she didn't die of natural causes after all, that means someone got to her despite the fact the hired help was on duty round the clock. Those guys who shot up the cottage you were in last night had no trouble breaching the resort's security." I shuddered involuntarily.

"All true. I would feel better if you'd come by and go through the house with me this afternoon. I'll have mighty mouth with me when I move in. Not much gets past Marlowe, but I'd like to know what else I can do to be sure the place is as secure as I can make it. Plus, I can fill you in on whatever I learn at the formal reading of the Will."

"Okay. Maybe we'll get lucky, and the guys in custody will give up something. We've requested search warrants to get information from the phones they had on them, as well as their credit cards and bank accounts. Murder for hire is usually a cash transaction, but if one or both made a cash deposit not long after your Aunt Lettie died, that might make it clearer that's why someone sent them after you. Now that I know who you are and what you're doing here, I'm going to go back over the report I wrote documenting my surveillance of the past few days. Who knows if a stop they made that didn't seem meaningful at the time might provide a tie-in to someone connected to you or your aunt."

"I appreciate anything you can do to make this nightmare go away. When I left LA, I thought the biggest challenge I'd face was burying my aunt. Do you think I should ask the funeral director about a two-for-the-price-of-one deal?" I stood up abruptly, trying to shake off the bout of fear that had gripped me. Austin reached out and took my arm.

"I'm happy to drive you to the meeting if you'd like."

"No. You've got plenty to do to help me figure this out as it is. This is probably a good time to get as much done as we can. You've got my would-be killers locked up, and whoever hired them is going to need a few days to regroup and come up with a new plan or hire someone new." I realized Austin still had his hand on my arm. I smiled at him. It had to have been an even longer night for him than it had been for me if he'd tracked down the gunmen after he left my cottage. Who knows what he'd gone through to do that and place them into custody. He had such a worried expression on his face that I felt sorry for him. "Some day off, huh?"

"My boss understands the importance of following up—what helps you, helps us throw the book at those two scumbags we're holding in lockup. She also knows I feel bad that we let those guys get as close as they did to shooting you. On or off-duty, I'm not going to let go until we've figured out who hired those thugs." It must have dawned on him that he still had a grip on my arm. He released me and returned my smile.

"Not something you mean quite so literally, I take it."

"It's not a bad idea. Maybe I should cuff us together." I laughed, surprised that it didn't sound half bad to me either.

"Now how would I explain that to Franklin Everett?"

"You're a black sheep, remember? And, as Denny Saunders put it, you do know how to make an entrance!"

"I won't be making any entrance at all if I don't shower and dress—and put on the power suit I bought to wear. I want black sheep to be the last thing Franklin Everett imagines me to be when I walk into my first meeting with him. Who knows who else will be in the room."

"I bet he'll have plenty on his mind when he sees you, and it won't have anything to do with you being a black sheep, either." Then he stood and pulled me close. "Don't take any chances, okay? Go straight to the meeting and then to your aunt's house where I'll join you." I leaned in and put both hands on his chest. His heart was thumping loudly. So was mine.

"I promise. Then, I'm taking you to dinner, and you can help me celebrate Aunt Lettie's legacy—whatever that turns out to be. I wish you could have met her. I bet you would have liked her." Austin put both hands over mine that were still pressed against his chest.

"I bet I would have, too, since I like her Calla Lily so much." I felt the two of us sliding into dangerous territory.

"Thanks, Marshal," I said as I gave him a peck on the cheek and then pushed him back. "Now get out of here so I can put on my game face."

4

The Will

I SHOWERED, DID my hair and makeup, and then put on the business suit I'd planned to wear. The charcoal grey skirt and jacket, along with a white blouse did what I wanted it to do—countered any image Franklin Everett might have in his mind that I was a Hollywood diva returning to make a scene or otherwise cause trouble. I had my hair pulled back into a chignon and kept the makeup light. A pair of sensible, black low-heeled pumps completed the look. I turned around in front of the full-length mirror on the back of the bedroom door and then put my hands on my hips.

"Calla Lily, what on earth are you doing?" I said aloud in my best mimicry of Aunt Lettie's voice. I was suddenly overwhelmed by the need to represent Aunt Lettie as the woman she was and had helped me become, even though she was gone. She'd march in there as a woman to be reckoned with, not as a shrinking violet hoping not to be any trouble to anyone.

"Time for plan 'B,'" I muttered as I slipped out of that suit and tossed it onto the bed. "If someone's gunning for me, I'm going to go down swinging!"

In minutes, I'd transformed myself. In a form-fitted, black V-neck, wool crepe sheath, I stood as tall as my five-foot-four-inch frame allowed in a pair of spiky six-inch heels. I kept the chignon but added bright red lipstick, a string of pearls, and a pair of matching earrings Aunt Lettie had given me when I graduated from college. They made her presence a tangible one. In a tailored coat and brimmed felt hat, I hoped I now conveyed the image of a woman used to commanding attention and getting her way.

"Don't mess with Calla Lily," I said, using Aunt Lettie's voice again and wagging my finger at myself in the mirror. Marlowe got the message. He yipped and turned around in a circle with the kind of glee that dogs exude so naturally.

"Come, Marlowe. Let's go raise a little ruckus if need be. If Austin is right, and there's someone with an ax to grind because Aunt Lettie left her house to us, we're going to find that out."

The drive from the resort to Franklin Everett's office in Calistoga took about twenty minutes. It was a scenic drive along a road that wound through vineyards and wineries—several with much more recognizable names than the Calla Lily Vineyards and Winery. The colors wouldn't be out in their full glory until October, but gold-tipped leaves on the vines sparkled in the morning sunshine. In among the greens, pinks, and purples of the grape leaves, there was plenty of color.

I glanced in my rear view mirror a couple of times hoping there was no truck stalking me. My Mercedes hybrid sedan has some miles on it. I keep it in tiptop shape since getting stranded in LA isn't something you want to have happen. My car is gutsier than it looks. In a pinch, I could step on it and make my way to the safety of the next winery or B&B or some other stop along this stretch of road.

"Unless they come after me with a frigging rocket launcher this time," I mumbled nonsensically. Marlowe, who was strapped into his doggie restraints in the back seat, must have thought I was speaking to him. He whined a little. "It's okay, boy; Mama's just a bit wackier than usual." Marlowe woofed, apparently agreeing with me.

That's when I noticed a car cruising some distance behind me. I hadn't seen it earlier, so it must have pulled onto the road from a shop or some other establishment I'd passed. Maybe someone who'd spent the night at a B&B or stopped for brunch as they meandered through wine country. They weren't meandering now. Whoever it was in the big Cadillac heading my way was in a hurry!

Hopefully, not in a hurry to catch up with me, I thought scanning the road ahead for someplace I could turn off if necessary. I sped up. The driver in the car behind me kept coming. When I checked in my rearview mirror again, I was shocked to see it had nearly caught up. My paranoia grew. Marlowe woofed again, then stood and tried to twist around in his seat. He barked and snarled.

With the Cadillac almost on my bumper now, I could tell the driver wasn't happy. For a second, there seemed to be something familiar about the angry man behind the wheel. I couldn't make out much, though, other than dark glasses and the teeth-gritting expression he wore. I breathed a little easier when a woman's hand reached over from the passenger seat and slapped him on the hand.

"It's okay, Marlowe. If they're having a spat, it's not likely to be another team of hired killers," I said aloud. "I should have said your Mama's a *lot* wackier than usual."

Even if I wasn't being stalked, whatever was going on behind me wasn't good. The driver had drifted toward the berm when the hand-slapping incident occurred. Now, he was doing the antsy weaving some people do when they're intent on passing a driver who's going too slowly. The curve in the road made passing impossible. As soon as I hit a straightaway, I pulled as far to the right as I could and slowed down a little. The driver blared his horn, pulled around, and cut in front of me. His brake lights came on as if he might slam to a stop. The gesture was a stupid, angry one given that he carried a carload of people. The back seat was full. I backed off even more; glad there wasn't anyone else on the road behind me.

A couple of minutes later, I heard more honking. As I navigated another curve in the two-lane roadway, I could see a plume of dust. A driver in the oncoming lane had pulled off the road and must have done so quickly to avoid a collision with the Cadillac that was now two cars ahead of me.

"I hope wherever he's going is worth this—and he gets his passengers there alive," I huffed.

In another ten minutes, I reached Calistoga. The town's not a very big one when compared to other towns and cities in the Napa and Sonoma Valleys. It had been a while since I'd been in Calistoga, but one of the virtues of small town living is that so little changes over time. After a couple of quick turns, I arrived at the offices of Franklin Everett and Associates. There couldn't be too many associates given the small size of the building. Like many commercial sites in small California towns, the offices were housed in what had once been a private residence.

The porch was inviting, although I doubt anyone ever used the comfy chairs set out on it. I followed a sign indicating that parking was in the rear. What must once have been a driveway alongside the home opened into a small paved lot instead of a backyard. There was room for half a dozen cars. Several spots were already occupied. The Cadillac sat in one of them. Marlowe growled.

"My sentiments exactly!" I said as I slid out of my seat, grabbed my purse and a leather portfolio I'd brought along to take notes and stash any paperwork the attorney might give me. In another minute, I had Marlowe on his leash and out of the car. A sidewalk led us around to the front entrance. When we reached the porch, I bent down, carried my little pooch up the steps, and waltzed into the waiting room.

"Welcome, Ms. Callahan, they're waiting for you." I glanced at a clock on the wall. It was two minutes to ten.

"Eager beavers," I muttered under my breath.

"I'm sorry, did you say something?" the receptionist asked as she stood and then motioned for me to follow her down a short hall. She must not have cared to hear what I'd said since she didn't give me time to repeat it. "Can I get you a cup of coffee, bottled water, or..." She paused for a second, looking me over, "Perrier or Evian?"

"No, thank you. It's kind of you to ask," I said peering

at her through the dark lenses of the sunglasses I still wore. When I entered the room, I spotted the driver of the Cadillac. I hadn't seen Eddie Callahan in almost two decades. Even now, up close, I don't believe I would have recognized him except that my mother was seated next to him. Beside her sat my half-sister and two half-brothers. I'd seen my mother and her children more recently, but the only one I was sure I could nail in a lineup was my mother. I felt, more than heard, a guttural response from Marlowe as he stared at the group seated on one side of a round conference table.

A man rose to greet me, but before he could utter a word, my mother scooted out of her chair. She scampered toward me all aflutter.

"How lovely to have all Aunt Lettie's nieces and nephews in one room together."

"Except for the fact that she's dead, of course." I missed which of Dorothy Callahan's male children had made the comment. What I didn't miss were the suppressed snickers that followed. I hoped they were meant for Dottie and not Lettie.

I was a split second away from placing Marlowe on the conference table and telling him to "sic 'em." When my mother made a grab for me—presumably, to do the air kiss thing she'd repeated often after seeing it done in LA, Marlowe snarled and then snapped at her. She jumped back.

"It's okay, Marlowe, she won't hurt you." More snickers came from the niece and nephews on the other side of the room. "He's not himself today," I explained without adding the "fortunately" aloud. I blew a kiss toward

Dottie, and she returned to her seat. Franklin Everett, who was at my side, introduced himself and pulled out a chair for me.

"Nice to meet you in person, Mr. Everett."

"Franklin, please, Ms. Callahan."

"It's Lily—if we're going to be on a first-name basis." I beamed a photo-op worthy smile at him as I slid the dark glasses off and made eye contact. "You're such a darling to organize this get-together for us. I can't tell you how grateful I am not to have to shoulder that responsibility on such a sad occasion."

He did what men often do when I go into glamor girl mode—he bumped into his receptionist as he backed up to allow me to sit. He wore a goofy grin too. Not Eddie Callahan, who was grim-faced again. His hands gripped the edge of the table as if he still held onto the steering wheel.

"I'm glad you all arrived in one piece after the incident on the road," I said. I was deliberately obscure about which incident. Eddie paled and let go of the table.

"We were running late," Dottie commented, a little defensively.

"I assumed as much." Then I turned to speak to two other men at the table who were new to me. "I'm sorry, but I don't believe we've met."

"Forgive me, Lily. I was going to introduce them next. These are your aunt's associates. Mitch Carlson, who's in charge of production at the Calla Lily Winery, and Alexander Davidson, who oversees financial matters pertaining to the vineyards and winery." Both men began to stand.

"Please, don't get up, gentlemen. I'm glad to meet two of the masterminds behind the wonderful Calla Lily wines being produced. I was amazed at the quality of the bottles Aunt Lettie left for me on her last visit. Congratulations, too, on the notice they received this year." I was laying it on a little thick, but I meant what I said.

"We wouldn't want to disappoint you by producing anything unworthy of your name." I saw heads snap up among the family members sitting across from me. I suspected that Alexander Davidson was playing with me. There may even have been a tinge of sarcasm in his words, but it was reassuring that Aunt Lettie had known him well enough to tell him the story behind the name on the label.

"I'm grateful to you for that. Aunt Lettie came up with that nickname for me as a term of endearment. Using it for the winery was a testament to how committed she was to the success of the venture. From all Aunt Lettie taught me over the years about the wine business, I appreciate how challenging it is to launch a small winery and keep it going. It's remarkable you've done that while not only increasing sales three or four percent a year but also improving the quality of the product. I'm sure much of the credit for the improvements in quality goes to you, Mr. Carlson, and what you've accomplished since you took the lead on the production side. Aunt Lettie raved about your uncanny sense as a winemaker." Both men were silent and appeared to be surprised by my statements. Mitch Carlson spoke first, with what sounded like sincerity.

"Lettie was a savvy woman, so it's a great compliment to hear she thought so highly of my efforts." Then Davidson put in his two cents worth.

"Your aunt appears to have kept you abreast of what goes on behind the scenes, too. That will make this transition easier than I—we—anticipated." A sudden furtiveness came over him. The pupils of his eyes had shrunk to tiny pinpoints as if to hide his inner thoughts.

Hmm, I wondered. *What transition was he anticipating and why had he expected it to be more difficult? More difficult than what?* The room had grown silent again. Rather than ask the questions that had popped into my head, I looked at Franklin, who was waiting patiently to carry out his responsibilities to Aunt Lettie.

"I'd love to hear more about what's going on at the winery, but I'm sure Franklin wants us to hear what Aunt Lettie has to say." He smiled. "You must be a very busy man, and we can't possibly be the only people scheduled to meet with you today."

His receptionist, who sat nearby, looked askance as if I might have that wrong. Perhaps, small town lawyers aren't crushed under the weight of the incessant demands placed on every lawyer I'd ever met in LA.

"By all means," Franklin said. "Let's proceed with the reading of the Will. It won't take long. Letitia Morgan's Last Will and Testament is as straightforward as she was. That includes a few surprises, as you might also expect, given her generous spirit." That set off a round of rustling from the family members in attendance.

The reading started off simple enough with the routine recitation of Lettie's name and address, and the declaration that this was, indeed, her Will, revoking all Wills and Codicils previously made. The first round of eyebrow-raising—mostly from me, to be honest—came in the forgiveness of debts. Aunt Lettie formally forgave unpaid loans in the total amount of one hundred fifty thousand dollars made to Dorothy Callahan. I was shocked since Lettie had never mentioned that she'd loaned money to my mother. Dottie was a little puzzled—I suppose it never occurred to her she needed forgiveness for debts owed to a dead woman.

Aunt Lettie also made provisions to continue to fund a private charitable foundation she'd recently established. The "Calla Lily Conservancy" funds projects aimed at protecting the local environment, including a college scholarship program for high school grads in the area with an interest in environmental studies. My aunt made it known that she hoped I'd take a leadership role and occupy a seat on the foundation's board, acknowledging the limits placed on my involvement by my career.

Clearly, Aunt Lettie wrote this Will before my career had taken a tumble toward oblivion. I was touched by her desire to have her good works continue even after her death and her faith in me to make that happen. My family members were either oblivious or unimpressed. Their eyes had glazed over. Except for Eddie Callahan who was on pins and needles awaiting what came next.

Gasps followed. The loudest came from family members when Franklin read that apart from specific bequests, Lettie had left the bulk of her estate to me which he estimated to be worth upward of fifty-million-dollars. I almost gasped, too. Franklin's off the record estimate caught me off guard even though Austin had tried to alert me to the possibility that my inheritance could be substantial.

Her legacy not only included the house and the land on which it was built but her residual personal property including cash, jewelry, and collectibles. Plus, the vineyards and her shares of the Calla Lily Vineyards and Winery, LLC. It was that last provision that inspired a tiny expression of air to escape from a non-family member—Alexander Davidson.

All eyes were on me. As an actress, you'd think I'd be used to that by now. Except for Franklin's kindly expression, the stares weren't anything close to those I get from appreciative fans. If my family members hadn't hired the killers that Austin held in confinement, they might be angry enough to do it now. Aunt Lettie had left them the means to pay for it, too, now that they had the cash given to them in the bequests!

Although I stood to inherit most of her estate, Lettie left specific bequests to several other people. That included gifts to my half-siblings, although she'd added a bit of a twist to the offers. They could each accept cash in the amount of fifty thousand dollars immediately or draw from a trust set up for each child to cover tuition, books, and living expenses to earn a four-year college degree. It would take about twenty seconds to figure out the second option represented maybe as much as ten times the value of that cash gift—depending on where each beneficiary chose to go to school. Pennywise-Pound Foolish won out!

Rose Callahan spoke up first. "What good will that do me? I already finished two years of college, and I'm not going back anytime soon. Check please!"

Her younger brothers, who looked to their parents for guidance, got the bad advice I'd expected Dottie and Eddie to offer.

"The future's uncertain, isn't it? If I were you, I'd take the money while you can."

Dottie uttered those words, but Eddie Callahan's head was bobbing up and down in enthusiastic agreement. Somehow, I doubt either nephew would ever see a dime. Rose was old enough to have the check written to her directly, but I bet the boys' gifts would end up in Dottie and Eddie's bank account. In any case, the matter was settled expeditiously.

That wasn't the only concern that had earned me those disapproving stares. Once the final provisions of the Will had been read, and family members had made their decisions about their bequests, Alexander Davidson spoke.

"Franklin, I must have misunderstood. I was under the impression that Lettie was going to sell her shares back to us and the cash value would be given to her beneficiary, not the ownership per se."

"Lettie mentioned you suggested that as an option, but upon further reflection, she decided not to change her Will." The room went silent as if waiting for an explosion. Alexander Davidson said nothing, but he was as white-knuckled as Eddie Callahan had been when he drove up behind me and then sped past me like a fiend.

What's up with that? I wondered as Marlowe shifted in my lap. Aunt Lettie hadn't raved about Davidson as she'd done about Carlson, but she'd never given me a reason to believe she had a problem with him or concerns about his business acumen. What did those white knuckles mean?

"There are a dozen other small bequests Lettie has made asking that specific items go to particular people. I can go over those with you, Lily, rather than take up everyone's time."

"Franklin, thank you so much for your help today. If there's nothing more we need to do as a group, I hope I can have a few minutes of your time alone." I smiled a pretty smile.

"Yes, we need to do that next. There are several issues to address so you can take possession of your aunt's home and finalize the transfer of her other assets to you." He turned to his receptionist and spoke to her quietly. She stood.

"If the members of the Callahan family, other than you, Lily, will come with me, please. I have paperwork we need to complete regarding the debt forgiveness and the bequests." They stood and filed out after her without another word to me. I had a sneaking suspicion, however, that I'd hear from them again now that Aunt Lettie had bequeathed her purse strings to me. What concerned me more, though, were the purse strings held by the gentleman in the expensive business suit getting ready to leave the room.

"Thanks for your participation today. I hope you'll let me know when the next board meeting will be held and how I can best prepare. I won't pretend that I can fill Aunt Lettie's shoes, but I'll do my best to fulfill my responsibilities in the way her legacy deserves." As I spoke, I realized I was most likely asking for more trouble. After almost being gunned down by two paid hitmen, how much more trouble could I be in?

5

Home Sweet Home

THERE'S NOTHING QUITE so eerie as a house in which someone has died. Even if it was death from so-called "natural causes." Death's not natural. It only seems that way because we ignore it as best we can. Some of us stick our heads in the sand like ostriches pretending if we don't see it, it can't see us. Others attempt to outrun it. Fast living will only kill you faster. As a refugee from the fast track, I ought to know.

After my little talk with Austin this morning, I realized Aunt Lettie's death probably saved my life. Hollywood's a cruel place for an actress who's closing in on thirty. Or, in my case, an actress looking at thirty in her rearview mirror. News that Aunt Lettie had left her property to me came the very same week I lost yet another bid for a television commercial and got an eviction notice from my condo in Westwood.

"Why me?" I'd asked Franklin Everett, too shocked to inquire further than that when he called to tell me the sad news about Aunt Lettie's death and my inheritance.

"I assume it's because you were her ward for so many

years. Your aunt left a letter for you. She might have more to say in it," Franklin Everett replied. "When we get together for the reading of the Will, I'll give it to you."

From one black sheep to another, my dear Calla Lily. Come home. I felt her presence—both comforting and guilt-inducing—as I read those words. Her note had more to say about her love for me, the happiness I'd brought her, and her hopes for me, too. My biggest hope was that I'd live long enough to find the happiness she yearned for me to have.

As I walked through the house, Marlowe's feet made little tapping sounds on the newly restored hardwood floors. Memories flooded my weary mind, along with sunlight that streamed in through a large picture window Aunt Lettie had installed in the parlor overlooking the wraparound porch. I was mesmerized, once again, by the sweeping vistas of the vineyards as they sloped down the hillside on which Lettie's house was built.

It had been years since I'd visited the strong, independent woman here. She never seemed to mind making the trips to tinsel town where I did my best to wow her with my Hollywood insider perks. Now, I felt certain she would have preferred having me here, especially during the holidays. I could hear her laughter mixed with mine as I stood in the large farmhouse kitchen. Aunt Lettie had enlarged the island in the center of the workspace and had replaced the wooden countertops with gorgeous granite.

In fact, she'd redone the entire kitchen, although the wooden "Home Sweet Home" plaque I'd made for her at school years ago still held a place of honor. Everything, even the restaurant quality appliances and an enormous extra prep sink she'd added, remained true to the kitchen's farmhouse roots, although ranch house might be more appropriate when speaking about Aunt Lettie's sprawling two-story Santa Barbara-style home. Her updates had given the kitchen a more continental flair like a home in Tuscany or the South of France, perhaps.

I ran my hands over the countertop where we'd gathered around baking bread, cookies, and other favorite recipes. Food was one of the only aspects of her southern heritage that she'd enthusiastically embraced. She loved Sliced Sweet Potato Pie with Molasses Whipped Cream, Sweet Alabama Pecan Bread, and a recipe a Kentucky friend had shared with her for a sweet, rich, silky Transparent Pie.

We'd made homemade jam with grapes from our vineyards and others with whom Aunt Lettie had traded. I almost broke down realizing I'd never hear her soft voice tinged by a southern upbringing she could never completely shake despite elocution lessons. Why had I waited so long to visit the woman who'd changed my life—saved it once already—all those years ago when my parents had reached the end of their rope with my wicked, rebellious behavior?

The weeks had turned into months and the months into years as I made myself at home with Aunt Lettie. At eighteen, my parents had requested that I return home. Aunt Lettie suggested, instead, that I go to college in California. By then, I had stars in my eyes. A local Summer Theater program had turned my angsty teenage attention-seeking into a passion to perform. All I wanted to do was go to Hollywood and become an actress. Aunt Lettie had humored me, spending a ton of money on music, voice, and dance lessons.

Attending the UCLA Performing Arts program had been an easy compromise—for me anyway. Maybe not so easy for Aunt Lettie, who would probably have been happier if I'd gone to college in San Francisco. I remembered the way she'd clung to me before returning home that fall quarter when classes began.

My parents were horrified when I told them about my plans. Hollywood is still Babylon to members of the supposedly staid side of the Alabama clan into which I was born. I'd finally given them proof that my inner black sheep had won out, as they'd feared all along. My mother's sister, Ruth, had called me livid that I was creating more trouble for my mother. I've suppressed her words, but she accused me of being a throwback to the bad blood that expressed itself when Tallulah Bankhead shocked everyone by announcing her intention to become a movie star.

"My family will have plenty to say about me when they get back to Montgomery now, won't they Marlowe?" He looked up at me from where I'd given him a snack.

Franklin Everett's receptionist had brought us lunch when the noon hour rolled around. I had a pile of papers to go through as Aunt Lettie's property changed hands. That included a truck and a car sitting in a garage that Lettie had rebuilt. Franklin had mentioned that my aunt made lots of changes since my last visit, but nothing that had adequately prepared me.

"Lettie's done lots of work on the house and grounds in the past few years. I believe she wanted everything to be perfect for you when you came home."

"What made her think I'd be coming home?" I'd wondered aloud.

"I can't be certain, but your aunt mentioned concerns about her health when I met with her this past year. She may have hoped you'd come home for other reasons, too." Franklin's eyes darted to the door of his office. Perhaps checking to see that it was closed. "She wasn't specific, but she was trying to sort out business matters, too. Given the way Alexander Davidson reacted to the reading of the Will today, I imagine she was trying to come to some agreement with him about your role. Maybe hers, too, since she asked me what was involved in selling her holdings or dissolving the Calla Lily partnership. I didn't press her about it. Your aunt was in her eighties and had learned she had heart trouble. I figured she was entitled to slow down a little. Did she ever ask you about taking on a formal role in the business in her stead?"

"No, but recently we did talk about the possibility that I might return to the area. Maybe that's what she had in mind even though she didn't bring up any of this." I'd paused to eat a bite of the salad Franklin's receptionist had brought me. "Now, of course, I wish I'd asked more questions or just come home sooner."

"Your Aunt Lettie was proud of all you accomplished. You made her a happy woman for so many years. She understood the demands your career placed on you." Her note to me said many of the same things. *Had he read it?* I wondered.

I hadn't checked upstairs to see what changes Aunt Lettie had made to the bedrooms. I didn't do it now because I didn't want to have to run for it if the doorbell rang. Before I left Franklin Everett's office, I'd done as I'd promised and called Austin. He hadn't answered the phone, so I left a message on his voice mail telling him I was on my way to the house.

Where is he? I wondered. *Why hasn't he called?*

"Stop it, Lily!" I said aloud. Marlowe tilted his head one way and then the other. "I told you, your momma's gone off the deep end. Someone in wine country wants me dead. Maybe a few more people now too, after the reading of the Will. We need that lawman to get here."

I'd been surprised by how many times Austin had popped into my head since he left my hotel room this morning. It's not as if I didn't have plenty on my mind. Still, his handsome face and broad smile had intruded repeatedly as it did now. I wondered how he got the small scar on his chin that kept his face from being too pretty. I imagined running my finger over it and then reaching up to touch his lips. I shook myself all over as if that would clear my head.

I idly opened the large refrigerator, grateful that Franklin had bought me lunch. It was empty except for a few bottles of Calla Lily Vineyards' Cabernet Sauvignon. I flinched involuntarily. Aunt Lettie would never have stored unopened bottles of red wine in her refrigerator. It wasn't a wine snob thing, it was the fact that wines—even whites—degrade if not cared for properly. That was hard on Lettie who'd come to develop a deep appreciation for how much work is required to make a good bottle of wine in the first place.

Aunt Lettie would never have stored the bottles upright, either. Corks dry out faster in a kitchen refrigerator as it is, and the wine always needs to be in contact with the cork to keep it moist. Dry corks shrink, making it easier for the wine to oxidize and deteriorate more rapidly.

Franklin said someone had gone into the house to clean after Aunt Lettie's body was removed. That explained why the refrigerator had been emptied of its contents other than a few condiments in the door. It didn't clear up my confusion about why the bottles of wine were in there. Perhaps, they'd been sitting on the counter nearby and whoever cleaned up wasn't sure what to do with them.

I pulled out the bottles and set them on the granite kitchen island. As I examined them, I noticed a black mark on one of the labels. Someone had circled a hazy spot on the front of one bottle. It marked a blurred spot as if the label had come off the printer with an imperfection in it. When I examined the second bottle, it appeared to be fine. Then I noticed there were two letters underlined, identifying misspelled words in the wine description. I was about to give up finding a problem with the third bottle when I noticed another mark. This one was on the back near the address. The zip code was missing a number.

"How odd," I said aloud, and then yelped when the doorbell rang. "Come on, Marlowe. Thank goodness, that must be the marshal." As I took a step, the toe of my shoe sent a scrap of something sliding over the tile floor. I bent down to find a chip of china. I immediately recognized it as a small piece from one of Aunt Lettie's favorite teacups. I set the fragment on the counter and hustled to answer the door.

"Well, it's about time you got here!" I announced moments later as I opened the door, but the man standing on the porch wasn't Austin Jennings.

6

An Old Flame

"JESSE, IS THAT you?" I asked once my heart quit pounding after I first feared I'd opened the door to a stranger. When I realized it was Jesse Hargrove, my heart did a little flip flop. The man who'd been my first serious boyfriend stood on the doorstep with an engaging smile on his face.

"Yes, it is. Have I changed that much?" He had, in fact, changed a good deal. In more than ten years, who wouldn't? Gray tinged his sideburns, and there were deep, hard lines in his rugged face. His dark eyes appeared even darker somehow. The changes weren't unattractive. Just different.

"Not much," I lied. "Except for the mustache." That had been the biggest shock, apart from the fact that he was here at all. I'd forgotten how tall Jesse was at eighteen, or perhaps he'd added a couple of inches in height since then. Marlowe stepped out onto the porch, sniffed him, and then greeted the man with a woof. Jesse bent down and picked up Marlowe.

"Hello, little fellow! What's your name?" Jesse asked,

holding him for a couple of seconds before placing him back down on the porch.

"Meet Marlowe," I replied.

"As in the detective?" he asked. I nodded. Then Jesse paused, took off the baseball cap he wore, and shoved it into a pocket of his flannel jacket. "You haven't changed a bit, Lily." He turned his head one way and then the other.

I wasn't sure how to respond. What he said wasn't true, of course. Actresses live in fear of even the most minute changes that accompany aging. I'm no different. Every wrinkle blared at me from the television screen as I approached and then passed thirty. As Jesse continued to examine me, I sighed. What could I say? There's only so much you can do with Botox and dermal fillers. I was about to give him a simple 'thank you' when he broke into an enormous smile and spoke again.

"That's not true. You were a pretty girl in high school, but you're a beautiful woman now. It's not like I haven't seen you since then on TV and in the news, but I wasn't sure if that's how you really looked given how easy it is to manipulate photos." He shrugged, stepped forward, and wrapped me in his arms. "Welcome home."

Beneath the plaid flannel jacket, Jesse's arms were like steel. He lifted me off my feet for a second before placing me back on the porch the way he'd done moments earlier with Marlowe. His mustache tickled as he brushed my cheek with a kiss. That made me laugh.

"Is everything okay here?" I jumped as if I'd just been caught with my hand in the cookie jar. Austin had come up onto the steps from somewhere, in a rush by the sound his boots made storming onto the porch.

"I'm fine, Austin. I was just saying hello to an old friend who paid me a surprise visit. Jesse Hargrove, this is Deputy U.S. Marshal Austin Jennings." I could have sworn Jesse's jaw clenched when I introduced the marshal. He held out his hand, and the two men gripped each other—a vice-like grip from the way it looked to me. They eyed each other as if sizing up each other.

"Why don't we go inside? I'm not sure what's in Aunt Lettie's kitchen, but if nothing else, I can always offer you a glass of wine."

"I'm sure you and Marshal Jennings must have business to attend to, and I need to get back to work. My crew is hard at work on cluster thinning to ensure we get the highest quality yield from our harvest."

"Your crew?" I asked, puzzled by his statement.

"Yes. Didn't Lettie tell you she hired me as the vineyard foreman last year?" He appeared to be disappointed. Was he upset with Aunt Lettie because she hadn't told me? Surely, he couldn't have imagined that my decision to come home had anything to do with him given Aunt Lettie's death. He appeared to be so bewildered and forlorn that I tried to find something to say that would make him feel better.

"She may have mentioned it. Forgive me, Jesse, I'm not firing on all pistons right now." He nodded. When he spoke again, it dawned on me that I wasn't the only one grieving my aunt's sudden death.

"I'm sorry about Lettie. I'm sure you'll miss her. We all will." Jesse shot a sideways glance at Austin in a way that might have meant "present company excluded." Then he put his baseball cap back on his head and tipped it at us. Austin responded using his big white Stetson.

"I guess you were right when you said you weren't going to be here alone," Austin said as he followed me into the foyer. I didn't realize he'd stopped until I reached the point at which the gleaming wood floors came to a crossroads. A winding staircase would take us to the second floor, while a hallway led in both directions on this one. I turned and responded to his comment as he shut the door behind him and then locked it.

"That's not quite what I meant, since, as you could probably tell, I didn't know Lettie had hired him to manage the vineyards. It's not bad, though, is it? Having an old friend around to keep an eye on things can't hurt," I offered.

"It depends what he's keeping an eye on. You can be a distraction, Calla Lily. That goes double if the old friend is still carrying a torch for you. Even if the flame's died down for you, it may not have for him." I wasn't sure what to make of Austin's tone or his comments that bordered on meddlesome. Who was he to say a word about my love life—past or present?

"Don't tell me that report about my past your boss put together includes information about a high school boy-friend!"

"No. I didn't need to read it in a report." His eyes traveled up and down my body as he walked toward me. "What happened to the business suit? Yeehaw, Miss Lily, you are a sight to behold!" He spoke in a mock voice like you might hear in an old western, took his Stetson off, and hit it against his thigh. Marlowe loved it. He spun around and then added the doggie equivalent of a yeehaw.

"Steady, cowboy!" I stepped toward him. "No distractions allowed. I need you to be completely focused to get me out of the mess I'm in."

"Sorry, ma'am, but if that's the case, please don't come any closer." Then he grinned. "Too late!" He reached out and pulled me into his arms. I laughed and struggled to wriggle free. He spoke again, his breath warm against my cheek.

"I couldn't stop thinking about you. I should never have let you out of my sight." My laughter ended as the mood turned more serious. I probably should have continued to push until I was free of his arms, but they were comforting after a grueling morning in a life that no longer made a bit of sense to me. A hitch caught in my voice when I spoke.

"Austin, when I say mess, I mean it." He hugged me tighter, and I put my head on his chest. "I'm in so much trouble!"

"Does that mean the reading of the Will was not uneventful?" Austin took the hand I'd rested on his chest, clenched it in one of his, and led me down the hallway. When we reached the doorway to Aunt Lettie's study, he stopped. I tugged him toward the kitchen as I responded to his question.

"Yes, I'd say so. This way. I'll tell you all about it, but I also want to show you something." I held onto his hand as we walked to the kitchen. His eyes roamed around the spacious room. He let go and went to a door that led out behind the house to an enormous green space that was more a meadow than a lawn. Aunt Lettie kept it mowed, but did little else to tame it. I noticed that my aunt had redone the redwood deck attached to the house and expanded the patio. The yard backed up to an even wilder fringe of brush that bordered a wooded area where a fence ran along the edge of my aunt's property separating it from the woods.

Austin scanned the area, and then reached in and pulled out a small pair of binoculars from a pocket inside his jacket. I thought I'd felt a gun when he'd held me close. Now, I saw it in a shoulder holster.

"Is that barbed wire along the top of the fence?"

"Yes. This was once the back pasture of a ranch, as I understand it. While I was growing up, there was a breach in the fence that my friends and I used to get into the woods. And before you ask, yes, it's been fixed. Aunt Lettie wanted to keep the deer away from the vineyards below. There's no easy way to get onto the property back there unless you want to risk getting a nasty cut from razor wire."

"What a place to call home!" Austin said as he tore his eyes from that pastoral view to gaze at the gleaming kitchen.

"It was. I don't ever remember feeling unsafe when my friends and I went exploring in the woods. My hand brushed the granite as I reached for one of the bottles of wine. "It wasn't nearly so magazine-worthy when I was growing up here. Aunt Lettie has really gone all out on a home improvement kick." Austin checked the locks. He opened the inside paneled door, checked to make sure the screen door was locked, then closed the door and locked it again.

"You need to add deadbolts here and on the front door. Are there other entrances into the house?"

"No."

"Where does this door lead?"

"The cellar where Lettie used to store the jams we made and canned goods. It used to be a real old-fashioned cellar with an ancient boiler style furnace and a dirt floor. Soon after I moved in, Aunt Lettie had the heating redone and added air conditioning. She redid the cellar then, too, creating a place to store wine." I stepped carefully through the door Austin had opened. A motion sensor light came on as I walked down wooden steps. Austin followed me.

"Wow!" He exclaimed when we reached the foot of the stairs. The low light revealed walls of wine stored on shelves. "How many bottles are down here? They can't all be from the Calla Lily Vineyards and Winery."

"No, they're not. I'm not sure how many bottles are down here. My aunt kept an inventory that must be on her laptop. She collected wines even before the vines here were old enough for her to take winemaking seriously. The fields were planted for over a decade before she began marketing the grapes. And it was years after that before she decided to try her hand at producing wine under her own label. The Calla Lily Vineyards and Winery is one of the things I want to discuss with you."

I reached out and adjusted a bottle here and there. The gesture was Lettie's. It reminded me of how much she'd relished teaching me about the different wines on the shelves. Even in the confines of this small space, I felt lost without her.

Austin had followed me as I wandered among the shelved bottles of wine. I must have conveyed my loss, somehow. When we got to the far wall, he reached out and embraced me again. This time I didn't pull away. In the cool, dimly lit corner of the cellar, I whispered to him.

"I couldn't stop thinking about you either," I confessed, feeling a little guilty about how often my fascination with Austin had intruded on my grief as it was doing now. He tipped my chin up and kissed me. A gentle, almost playful kiss, I was moved by a rush of emotion that turned the kiss into something more urgent. It would be a relief to ditch the grief about Aunt Lettie's death and squelch the terror I felt about being caught up in a real-life whodunit where I was cast as the murder victim.

Why not get lost in the far more enticing mystery of discovering what more there was to learn about the marshal? I thought as I leaned in and pressed my body against him. Fortunately, the doorbell rang bringing me instantly to my senses. I grabbed a bottle of wine from a shelf behind Austin as he released me.

"Uh, oh," he said. "I bet your old flame is back."

"Don't worry," I said as I stood on my toes and spoke with my lips brushing his cheek. "There's a new marshal in town."

When we returned to the kitchen, I set the dusty bottle of Calla Lily Cabernet Sauvignon on the island next to the others that were already there. Austin appeared puzzled.

"You don't have to get me drunk to have your way with me," Austin said, wearing a slightly crooked smile.

"That's not what I'm doing," I said. "I'm after your mind, not your body." I click-clicked my way down the hall. This time as Austin followed, he checked each of the rooms we'd passed on our way into the kitchen. Some of them I hardly recognized. Aunt Lettie's dining room could be reached through a butler's pantry now. That had been a plain old pantry when I was growing up.

The powder room on the first floor was now palatial by comparison to the way it had once looked. The décor in Aunt Lettie's den had completely transformed it. I'd spent hours doing my homework while my aunt sat at her desk going over the accounts she kept. She did her accounting the old-fashioned way when I first arrived at age twelve, poring over ledger books, entering figures from receipts.

One night I told her how much easier it would be to keep her accounts on a computer, and how much I could use one for school. Within a week, she had someone in there to set one up. For the next few weeks, she devoted herself to mastering the basics of spreadsheets and never looked back.

"Calla Lily, you're a genius," she'd said once she had the hang of it. "There's just one problem, child."

"What?" I'd asked.

"You need one all to yourself. Happy early birthday!" It wasn't anywhere near my birthday, but I smiled even now remembering how much it had meant to me. I felt like a grown up sitting in the room working on my computer as she worked on hers. Now the room was more a library than a den, although a flat screen TV hung on one wall. Her desk was gone, and chairs were set up near the windows to take in the view.

In the dining room, I could hardly tell what had been changed apart from the interesting paint finish that had been applied to the walls. The room was full of stuff. Someone had started wrapping some items, but others, like a painting by Ruth Westphal—a plein air painter Aunt Lettie adored—leaned against a dining chair. When Austin poked his head in and looked around, it suddenly hit me.

"Those must be items Aunt Lettie identified as property to be distributed through her individual bequests." As I continued to the door, I explained what I meant by that. I reached for the door handle as the doorbell rang a third time.

"Just a minute!" I called out as I fiddled with the lock. In a quieter voice, I spoke to Austin. "What I don't understand is how someone could have known what personal property Aunt Lettie intended to pass on to individuals. Franklin gave me a copy of the Will that includes the bequests, but that just happened today. He offered to have his receptionist help me handle them."

Austin peeked out of a curtained window next to the door. I had a flashback to the way he'd done something similar at the cottage and found myself transported back into that combat zone. I froze.

"It's okay," he whispered and then opened his jacket. "If your visitor makes one wrong move, I've got you covered." When I opened the door, I shook my head at Austin. All I needed was for him to toy with me as wired as I was! He wasn't going to get another kiss any time soon. He smiled. My resolve melted.

"Come in, Judy!" The dark-haired woman in jeans and a bright red jacket stepped into the house and looked around. I shut and locked the door behind her. When her eyes came to rest on Austin, she checked him out from the top of his head to the tips of his pointy cowboy boots. I must have appeared a little shocked because she shrugged.

"You never get too old to look, honey. Lettie must have taught you that. No wonder it took you so long to answer the door. I brought you food. After they took your aunt's body to the morgue, I came back here and cleaned out the refrigerator, so I know there's nothing to eat. You can share it with handsome." With that, she winked at Austin and then took off for the kitchen with the casserole she was carrying. She also had a brown paper bag hanging off one arm.

"I don't mind being called handsome, but most people call me Austin." Austin had caught up with her as she sped down the hall in a pair of the work boots Judy often wore. A hardworking woman, she runs an antique shop set up in what was once her barn. Most days she got up and did more chores before the shop opened at nine a.m. than I did all day long. She kept chickens, had goats, grew an herb garden, and who knows what else.

"Judy Tucker is—was—one of Aunt Lettie's best friends, Austin." I had to holler since the two of them had already reached the kitchen. "Come on, Marlowe. I have a few questions for Judy, don't you?"

As Marlowe and I stepped toward the kitchen, I stopped. The truck Jesse had parked in my driveway earlier zipped by as if he'd just left the driveway. *Where had he come from?* I wondered. Surely, he hadn't been sitting out there since he'd said goodbye earlier. Wouldn't I have seen his truck when I passed the picture window in the parlor given where he was parked when I met him on the porch?

"Let's ask Judy if she happened to bump into my old flame on her way in here, okay, Marlowe?"

7

Natural Causes

WHEN I WALKED into the kitchen, it was Austin's turn to flinch as if I'd caught him with his hand in a cookie jar—because I had. He was sitting on a barstool, with half a dozen cookies on a plate, pulling another one from the open container in front of him. Judy was pouring him a glass of milk.

"Fresh baked cookies and farm fresh milk, too! Can you believe it? This is the best chocolate chip cookie I've ever eaten. Come, sit here and try one."

"She's had lots of them. I made them the way you and Lettie used to bake them." Judy handed Austin a glass of milk. He drank about half of it to wash down the cookie he'd stuffed into his mouth.

"You know how to bake these?" Austin asked with something akin to wonder in his voice. "Anytime you want?"

"Yes, I do. I lack self-control, so I don't bake them often unless I have someplace to take them," I replied slipping into a seat next to him. It hadn't been that long since I'd had lunch, but who could refuse cookies and milk? I started to grab a cookie from Austin's plate, and he moved the dish away.

"These are mine. I bet if you're nice to Judy, she'll find one of these sparkly glass plates for you."

"The way to a man's heart is through his stomach," Judy said as she pulled another dessert plate from the cupboard. When she set it on the counter, she moved the little piece of china I'd found on the floor earlier.

"I thought I found all the pieces when I cleaned up. I tried to save them in case they warrant a closer look, depending on what the coroner says once she gets the tox screen back."

"What?" I asked. Austin had tried to say something too, but he hadn't swallowed before he spoke and choked. I was on the verge of taking measures to resuscitate him when he caught his breath.

"Aren't you the least bit suspicious that your aunt up and died like she did?" Judy asked.

"Yes. I was, even before the trouble I ran into last night. That's when Austin and I met."

"I figured the marshal had something to do with the shootout at the resort. When I ran into Jesse, he told me you must still be worried because you had the law with you." She smiled. "I wasn't sure what to believe. Jesse's no fan of law enforcement since he stepped out of line a while back."

"What? Cookies, please. This is all so overwhelming that I don't know where to begin."

"Sugar will pick you right up. The milk will calm you down, too, like it did when you were a young thing. She was so cute even then." I put my head in my hands.

"Does everyone know someone tried to kill me?"

"Not everyone. I have a cousin who works at the resort, and she told me you were almost killed during an attempted robbery. She said the thieves were after the Emmy Award you won. I knew that wasn't true since it's upstairs on the mantle in Lettie's room. What were they after?"

"The marshal has the culprits in custody, but no one knows for sure what they were doing. What do you mean when you say that Jesse stepped out of line?"

"Jesse probably wants to tell you himself since he's hot on the idea of you two picking up where you left off." Austin gave me a "told you so" nod.

"How can that be? I haven't seen or spoken to him for almost fifteen years. We were kids—and headed in different directions even then." Judy shrugged and shook her head.

"I told him that when he got out on parole."

"Parole?"

"Shoot! Yeah, Jesse got busted growing weed. Half the farmers around here were dabbling in it, hoping to cash in when the law changed allowing sales of marihuana for recreational as well as medical use. He got a little ahead of the law and got caught red-handed. Anyway, when he got out of prison, Lettie hired him, and he was intent on getting in touch with you. She wouldn't give him your address or phone number but agreed to tell you that he was back in town and working as the vineyard foreman. Jesse said you seemed surprised that he was here, and figures Lettie let him down."

"Maybe she mentioned it. I had so much on my mind

when she visited me—I must have missed a lot. Aunt Lettie didn't say a word about a heart condition. She didn't seem sick either. I asked Franklin about having an autopsy done on Aunt Lettie, and he said he thought it could be arranged, but it needed to happen soon. Are you saying that it's already been done?"

"Yes. Doctor Hennessey asked for one—after I told him that he ought to be a little concerned that he got Lettie's heart condition so wrong. The EMTs that came out here said Lettie died from a heart attack. Since no one was with her at the time of her death and it happened so suddenly, the coroner probably would have done an autopsy anyway. I wanted to get it done without a delay, so I called Lettie's doctor and told him to make the request right away. That way it was on record before they removed Lettie's body."

"Franklin told Lily her aunt was being treated for a heart condition, so what was off about the EMTs conclusion that she died from a heart attack?" Judy put the lid on the milk and stowed it in the refrigerator before answering Austin's question.

"It hadn't been more than a few weeks since she was in the doctor's office for a checkup. He's been treating her for heart failure. He told her it was in the early stages and gave her a prescription for digoxin. I'm not surprised she didn't bring it up, Lily, since the doc said she'd probably outlive him. That's one reason I was suspicious when she suddenly dropped dead."

"I saw the police report, and it didn't say anything about foul play," Austin said.

"The police report? When did that happen?" I asked.

"While you were at your meeting with Franklin Everett. I told you I was going to check on a few things. That's one of them. It doesn't say much other than she was found dead, alone in her home from a suspected heart attack. Is that inconsistent with the findings from the autopsy?"

"No. The coroner's preliminary report says Lettie died from cardiac arrest. That could be what the EMTs meant when they said heart attack. The coroner also said there was something odd about the amount of digoxin in Lettie's system and she sent a blood sample to an outside lab asking for a more thorough tox screen. It ought to come back in the next day or two."

"What does odd mean?" I asked.

"She wouldn't say—not until she gets the lab results. There were also traces of a sedative found in Lettie's system. I'm the one who thought that was odd. Lettie would never have taken a sedative. I came over here the next day and went through Lettie's medicine cabinet—nothing! I was here to clean up, but that's when I got the idea to save the broken teacup. What if Lettie was doped up? If there's residue from the sedative on the pieces of the teacup, maybe it'll match what turns up in the lab results."

"It's too bad you didn't have a sample of the tea. That would be more likely to retain traces of the sedative than the cup. It depends on what was used, though."

"I guess you got one of those lectures at college about what to do if you suspect someone spiked your drink," Judy suggested.

"Not just at college. I was careful what I drank at Hollywood parties too. Never, never drink anything from a punchbowl. I also read up more recently on the use of knockout drugs when my character, Andra, used them to set up a lover for blackmail after he went back to his wife."

"I should have known. Andra was a nasty one," Judy said. "When I found your aunt, I didn't know about the sedative issue yet. There was something that didn't seem right to me from the get-go. She was on the floor here, but the cup was broken on the floor there. That didn't seem right to me. Or maybe it was the way she was facing— away from where the cup had fallen. I wondered if someone had moved her or the cup. I couldn't find her phone, either. When I came back to clean the next day, it was sitting on the counter near the sink. I may be getting on a bit—call the chickens or the goats by the wrong name and all that, but I wouldn't have missed something I'd spent half an hour hunting for."

"I don't understand the point you're making about the teacup and where it was in relation to Aunt Lettie's body. As her heart gave out, she could have dropped the cup and then took a couple of steps before she fell. Or maybe she fell, and the cup went flying."

"I'm probably not explaining it very well. I insisted Officer Benchley take pictures. Why don't you look at them, Austin, and see if you can figure out what's wrong? I was in shock at the time so it could be me."

"You sound like you were incredibly observant— especially under the circumstances. She was your friend. Aunt Lettie always said you had the makings of a master sleuth." I leaned in to give Judy a reassuring pat on her rough, working woman's hands. She clasped my hand and gave it a squeeze.

"When I retire, I don't know that I'll take up sleuthing, but I might write mysteries. Let's solve this real one, though, first. I'd bet money that your aunt didn't die from natural causes. Did you get the scoop about the Will from Franklin?"

"Boy, did I! I haven't had a chance to tell Austin about how weird it was. Lots of the bizarreness had to do with my family members, but not all of it. I believe my relatives were expecting to come away with more, although they didn't hesitate to take the cash Aunt Lettie offered each of my half-siblings."

"Modest bequests compared to what she left for some of us. I didn't want a stranger to paw through Lettie's special possessions, so I've gone through the copy of the list she gave me. They're all set out in the dining room. She left the Ruth Westphal to me, but I didn't want to take it until you knew what was going on."

"I wondered who'd done that. Thank you so much." I gave her hand another squeeze. "I would have had trouble finding the items she intended as gifts. Everything has changed so much here. I haven't even been upstairs yet. Did Aunt Lettie revamp that, too?"

"Oh, yes. Once Lettie got the bug to give you the option to use the place as a B&B, she redid just about everything."

"A B&B—for me?"

"Lettie was such a go-getter. The wine business is dicey, so she wanted another way to bring in money. She's been working on the development of a line of Calla Lily Food products, too—baked goods, jams, jellies, and preserves. Maybe these cookies." Judy nodded at Austin as she said that. "When your character was killed off, she hoped she could entice you to come home with the idea of running the B&B, doing acting workshops, and putting on plays in an outdoor theater."

"You've got to be kidding."

"No, I'm not. Wait until you see it! She had it built on a slope up here above the vineyards near where you and your friends used to put on plays for us. Guests can park here at the house and walk to the theater, but there's also an entrance off the main road that leads up here. That needs to be finished, and a gate needs to be installed."

Judy's latest revelation was more than I could bear after the pendulum swings my life had taken recently. It's as if my heart sprang a leak and filled my eyes with tears that rolled down my cheeks. Aunt Lettie's incredible thoughtfulness was beyond belief. It stood out in such stark contrast to my grasping relatives, the possibility that the precious woman might not have died of natural causes after all, and the fact that someone had sent hired thugs to shoot me! Judy handed me a tissue from a box on a shelf below her in the kitchen island.

"Why didn't she tell me?"

"Your aunt wanted you to figure out what you were going to do about your career. Plus, she wanted everything to be perfect for you before she revealed her latest masterpiece. That's how she was, you know?" Judy had tears in her eyes, too.

"I do know. It's going to be hard to get along without her, isn't it?" I asked.

"Yes. We'll help each other get through it. Right now, we've got to keep focused on finding out what happened to Lettie and who's responsible if it turns out her heart didn't just give out on her."

"When you found Aunt Lettie's phone, did you see calls from anyone that day? Did she have appointments with contractors or other visitors?"

"Not that I could see. I was a little surprised that Carol Matheson hadn't dropped by. She's a pleasant young woman who's a home health care nurse. Lettie hired Carol after her heart failure diagnosis. That should have been Carol's day to visit, but I didn't find any phone calls or texts between them. There wasn't anything about an appointment on Lettie's calendar either. I intend to call Carol and ask her about it."

"That's a good idea. Maybe Aunt Lettie canceled their appointment because she'd decided to meet with someone else that day and mentioned who that was to the nurse." Austin had been so quiet that I wondered if he'd fallen into a cookie-induced stupor of some kind. "What do you think, Austin? Does this all sound suspicious to you or are Judy and I just overreacting because of our loss?"

"There's definitely something going on. The drug stuff alone makes your aunt's death a suspicious one in my book. Was she having any trouble with anyone?"

"Besides the usual wrestling match with the boys on the Calla Lily Winery board you mean?" Judy asked.

"As in Alexander Davidson?" His image had popped into my head immediately.

"For one. He has a couple of cronies on the board who always stand by him no matter what he says, so them, too."

"Who is he?" Austin asked.

"He's the reason I said my family wasn't the only source of weirdness at the reading of the Will today. Apparently, Alexander Davidson, Calla Lily Winery's finance person, was under the impression that Aunt Lettie was going to sell her shares to the partners and leave me the cash rather than the voting shares and her seat on the board."

"That's the kind of thing I'm talking about," Judy said. "It didn't start out as a conversation about her Will, either. She wanted to bring you into the business when you came home—splitting her shares with you, so you could each have a seat on the board with voting rights. Lettie held a controlling interest in the partnership, and if she split her shares with you, the control would remain within the family if you two saw eye-to-eye on an issue. If not, so be it. She was ready to turn over some of the decision making to you. Alexander Davidson was strongly opposed to the idea from the moment she brought it up. He and a couple of others went to work on her. Not only did they oppose the idea of bringing you into the company now, but they urged her to change her Will, too."

"If they thought they'd succeeded in doing that, maybe they drugged Aunt Lettie with sedatives and caused her heart to fail so they could get control of her shares," I suggested as impossible as the idea sounded as the words came out of my mouth. If Aunt Lettie hadn't died of natural causes, someone had it in for her.

"Or maybe someone on the board found out she hadn't done that and paid to have you killed," Austin added. "Maybe Alexander Davidson wasn't as surprised as he pretended to be today when Franklin Everett read the Will."

"That could be true—especially if he was trying to cover his tracks after his hired help failed to do their job last night." I shook my head in disgust.

"Is that what happened at the resort? It wasn't a robbery?" Judy asked.

"Yes. Apparently, someone wants me dead. They were willing to pay pros to do it, too. They might have succeeded if Austin hadn't been stalking them while they stalked me. What I don't understand is why Alexander Davidson or anyone else would be desperate enough to kill Aunt Lettie or me to keep us off the board."

"I don't know if it's a motive for murder, but it's obvious Lettie and the management of the winery didn't always see eye-to-eye. Because of the number of shares she owned, she usually got her way. Maybe someone was fed up with her stubbornness," Judy replied.

"Why now? Over the years, I've heard her arguing on the phone with one manager or another, many times—with board members, too."

"If Alexander Davidson is power mad, Judy could be right that he was sick of sharing control with your aunt. Once she made it clear she wanted to involve you, the idea that he wouldn't call the shots even after Lettie was dead, could have pushed him off the deep end. Another possibility is that he's desperate to get control because he's up to no good."

"When I saw Aunt Lettie recently, she said she was at odds with some board members about how fast to grow the business without cutting corners on quality. Nothing in what she said about the debate suggested she feared for her life," I said.

"Lettie was concerned when someone suggested they buy wine from other vineyards to mix with those from the Calla Lily vineyards to increase production. I didn't think she was being unreasonable when she agreed to go along with the idea if they marketed the wines using different labels. That wasn't the only issue, although they might be related." Judy reached over and picked up one of the bottles of wine I'd removed from the refrigerator earlier.

"I wasn't sure how soon you'd want to step into the fray around business matters given that Lettie isn't even buried yet, but I didn't want you to be caught off guard. Someone at the winery left these bottles in a bag next to Lettie's car a few days ago. Lettie spotted the problems on the labels and confronted Mitch Carlson about it. He said he didn't know what was going on and referred her to the marketing folks. It's more than a problem with the labels, though. The wine's not a Calla Lily product."

"Are you talking about wine fraud?" Austin asked.

"Yes. Not a very good fraud either. She said the wine in the bottle she opened was dreadful. Lettie intended to bring the matter up at the next board meeting before reporting the problem to the authorities. In the meantime, she'd planned to hire a private investigator, hoping to get to the bottom of it."

"I guess that answers my 'why now' question, doesn't it? Could this get any worse?" I asked, shaking my head in disbelief. Just then, Austin's phone rang.

"Hello, Rikki," he said when he answered the call. "Lily's okay—she's sitting right here. What's happened?" Their chat wasn't a long one, and I couldn't hear what was being said on the other end. Austin's somber tone was enough to put me on edge. When he mentioned Calistoga and police, my stomach did a little flip-flop.

"Okay, thanks for the heads up. We'll check it out," Austin said.

"Check out what?" Judy and I asked almost at the same time.

8

An Unnatural Death

"WELL THERE'S NO doubt that this was an unnatural death," Judy whispered under her breath as we caught a glimpse of what was going on in Franklin Everett's office. I felt woozy and regretted the impulse that had brought us here. As soon as Austin had ended his call with Rikki Havens, I'd confronted him.

"I heard you say something about a police investigation underway in Calistoga. Is it at Franklin Everett's address?" I'd asked him that question, even though I knew the answer before Austin had nodded in agreement. "So, why call us?"

"Someone killed Franklin Everett. One of the dispatchers in our office picked up the police call. She alerted Rikki wondering if it had anything to do with the investigation into the shootout at the resort last night. Rikki said no but then grew concerned that it had something to do with another attempt on your life. Two violent episodes, on consecutive nights and only a few miles apart, is an unusual occurrence around here. She called to ask where you were."

"Okay," I said. "Your conversation was a little longer than that. Does she still believe it has something to do with me?"

"The police have questions for you." Austin had replied with a troubled expression on his face.

"Me? Why?"

"You were a visitor at his office earlier in the day, so you're on the 'to be interviewed' list." My throat went dry and my heart revved up as another layer of stress tumbled on top of the emotional rubble left in the wake of seemingly relentless events. That's when I was struck by the impulse to act.

"I'm not going to wait around stewing about it. If I'm 'to be interviewed,' let them ask their questions and get this nightmare over!"

"I didn't say the police wanted to ask you questions now. The last thing they want is for us to show up, unannounced, at a crime scene."

"Call them if you feel like it," I added irritably. "I'm going to pay them a visit—surprise or not!"

"I'm with Lily, so let's go. I have a few questions for the police, too. Because Franklin wasn't killed during another attempt on Lily's life doesn't mean his murder isn't about Lily and Lettie. I want to make sure they're conducting a proper investigation given his untimely death on the day the provisions of Lettie's Last Will and Testament were revealed." Judy was on the go. Austin stood there with his arms folded across his chest. He gave in when I met his gaze with a steely determination in my eyes.

"Don't kick them in the shins and get arrested if they

say no, promise?" Austin asked shaking his head. For some reason, the idea made me smile, not that I'd ever dream of doing such a thing.

"No kicking or screaming. Scout's honor!" I said as I waited on the porch for Austin to pass so I could lock the door.

"If they won't let us in or answer our questions, we'll turn around and come back here." Judy already had her keys out. Apparently, she was driving.

That conversation hadn't occurred much more than twenty minutes ago. Twenty minutes spent mostly in silence while I tried to come to grips with the fact that there'd been another death. I should have spent more time preparing for the grisly way in which he'd died, but murder and mayhem are new to me—offscreen anyway.

I felt shaky and stared at the items scattered all over the floor to avoid the horrific sight. It was too late, though. The image of Franklin Everett slumped at his desk was imprinted on my brain. Blood was pooled on the papers beneath him, spattered on the wall behind him, and elsewhere.

"Head wounds bleed a lot," Judy informed me. "I'm guessing he was hit more than once before he died."

"Very observant," a woman said as she joined us. She wasn't in uniform, but as she walked toward us, I spotted a star pinned at her waist. She wore dark brown slacks and a blazer in a lighter shade of brown. That had been a mistake since there was a smear of blood on a sleeve near one of the latex gloves she had on.

"Excuse me if I don't shake hands. I'm Deputy Dahlia Ahern with the Napa County Sheriff's Department.

Multiple blows, yes. I'd say the first blow might have been intended to get him to cooperate since it didn't kill him. It probably knocked him out. The initial wound bled like a son of a gun, but I doubt he felt the blows that followed later when his visitor finished him off."

"His killer went through his files, too, huh?" Judy asked.

"That appears to be the case." Her eyes wandered from Judy to me to Austin who was standing behind us.

"What brings you here, Austin? Our dead guy doesn't have a record. Do you have a lead on his killer? Please tell me it's a fugitive you're pursuing, and you know where the psychopath who did this is headed?" Austin shook his head. "Who are your friends, then, and why are they here?" Before he could speak a uniformed officer in the room dashed over to us.

"I let them all in," she said. "This is Judy Tucker. She's the woman who reported the death of Letitia Morgan to our department several days ago. This is Lillian Callahan, Letitia Morgan's niece who was here this morning for a meeting with Franklin Everett." She pointed me out and then continued to explain. "Beth Varner says Ms. Callahan was wearing a pair of sunglasses just like this one when she came in for her meeting with her aunt's lawyer. I hope Ms. Callahan can tell us more about what happened here."

"This is Officer Barbara Benchley—the Calistoga police officer I mentioned to you earlier who helped me with Lettie," Judy said. Officer Benchley was holding a clear plastic bag containing a pair of sunglasses that appeared to be the ones I'd worn this morning.

"Those do appear to be mine. I'm sure Beth Varner told you that when I met with Franklin earlier today, it wasn't here in his office." Both police officers were staring at me now. "I have no idea what happened, but I'm as eager as you are to find out. I left right after lunch. Twelve-thirty, maybe. I made a phone call as soon as I got to my car so I can give you a more precise time if you'd like me to check. When was Franklin killed?"

Officer Benchley pursed her lips as if doubting what I said. Or she could have been poised to deliver a tough cop line like, "We ask the questions, not you." As Andra, I'd been spoken to that way many times during her conniving career as a TV soap hellion. If that's what Officer Benchley was about to do, she missed her cue. Austin had a question.

"Where's his receptionist, Dahlia? I'm sure she can tell you where Franklin Everett met with Lily and when she left."

"We asked. What she can't tell us is how Lily's sunglasses got in here with Franklin. Can you?" Officer Benchley was indeed in tough cop mode.

"No. The last place I'm certain I had my sunglasses was when I took them off as I sat down at a conference table waiting for Franklin Everett to read my aunt's Last Will and Testament. The situation was a trying one, as I'm sure you can imagine, Officer Benchley. Keeping tabs on my sunglasses wasn't a priority. I may have left them in the conference room or in the small alcove area where Franklin and I met after that. As I said, I left here around half past twelve. It appears to me my aunt's lawyer was killed more recently. Am I wrong?"

"Even if you left when you say you did, that doesn't mean you didn't come back. Beth stepped out to run a couple of errands, but Franklin could have let you in. Maybe you left the sunglasses behind as an excuse to return."

"And then left them where you could find them, so you'd be sure to know I'd killed him? I'm not a very sneaky cutthroat, am I?" Austin cleared his throat. "Austin can tell you where I was after that."

"He can?" Dahlia asked. By the way she was quizzing him, I wondered if Austin had a history with this woman who was also named after a flower. I'm not sure why it bothered me given Jesse's unannounced visit a while ago. Maybe it was the amused look in Dahlia's eye. *Was Austin a player?* I wondered. I inched away from Austin in an almost imperceptible way—more inside than out, perhaps.

"Yes, he can," Judy said. "So can I, Barb. You're headed down the wrong path. I told you Lettie's death didn't sit right with me. Now her lawyer turns up dead after Austin had to rescue Lily from paid assassins last night. Lily hasn't been back long enough to plot Franklin's murder. Lettie was already dead, and Lily certainly didn't pay hired guns to try to kill herself. There's your psychopath—two of them in fact." Judy was exasperated.

"Except they're already under lock and key, aren't they, Marshal?" Dahlia asked. "We found that out when the Napa County Sheriff's Department got a dozen calls worrying that a drug war had broken out in the woods near Miller's Creek. By the time we got to the scene, we heard you'd taken off and rounded up the bad guys as soon as Rikki Havens sent in local police as back-up."

"This wasn't the work of a pro," Austin commented in a low voice. "This is personal—an angry, personal attack. That doesn't mean I'm as certain as you are, Judy, that this is about Lettie or Lily." I spoke before I could stop myself.

"I am, Austin. It's no coincidence this occurred so soon after my meeting with Franklin or that I'm implicated in the man's murder. Dahlia's got the psychopath thing right, though. No one in their right mind would have bludgeoned Franklin to death before getting what they wanted from his files first."

"What makes you so sure they didn't get what they were looking for?" Officer Benchley asked in a tone of voice that made it obvious that she wasn't done with me yet.

"The search was done as furiously as the bludgeoning, don't you think?" I asked. "The office has been ransacked."

"I should have taken that into account," Judy said. "Murder for hire is cold-blooded. This is bloodthirsty— desperate and angry like Austin said. Even more loosey-goosey than poisoning someone with an overdose of medication, isn't it?" She looked at Austin and me when she asked that question. Dahlia and Officer Benchley peered at us. They both opened their mouths as if to speak. If they were going to object to the conclusion Judy had reached about my aunt's death, they could wait because I had more to say.

"Trashing Franklin's office could also be a way to cover up what the person was searching for, but that doesn't cover the murderous rage, does it? Or the lame effort to cast suspicion on me. My now defunct character, Andra Weis, was no professional criminal, but she was an organized psychopath. Someone like that would have done everything in a much more thoughtful, methodical way. Whoever murdered Franklin lost control."

"I agree. Even if the events are somehow connected, I'm doubtful this vicious DIY job was done by the same person who paid hitmen to shoot you." Dahlia shrugged.

"I'm sure it's too soon to know what's missing—if anything." I wondered if, in fact, they'd ever be able to figure out what was or wasn't missing in this mess. The one man who could have helped put it all together again was dead.

"You're right about that. Just like it's too soon to know how many maniacs are behind the carnage un-leashed in our happy valley. Or how much of it has something to do with your homecoming, Lily. Once we finish collecting evidence and the coroner removes the body, we'll ask Beth Varner to see if she can tell if any-thing has been taken."

"Or destroyed," I added.

"That too," Dahlia agreed, as she scanned the floor. "Plenty of the paperwork dumped from Franklin's files has been ruined. So, yes, maybe Beth can make sense out of what the person was intent on destroying, even if nothing's been stolen."

"That could take days!" Judy exclaimed.

"If we're lucky. What's your point?" Dahlia asked.

"The killer's still out there! What if the person goes after someone else?" Judy was irate.

"Or gets away," I added.

"As I see it, this is a reason for you both to lay low while we get a handle on what's gone on here. I'd like to drop by and have a longer conversation about the crime spree underway. Gunfire, an intentional drug overdose, and now a bludgeoning death. I'd like to believe they're all connected—maybe it's just wishful thinking that if we solve one crime, we'll solve them all. Anyway, I'd like to hear what you believe it's about."

"Why not? If you come by my Aunt's house at the Calla Lily Vineyards by seven, you can have dinner with us." Both Austin and Judy appeared ready to object.

"I'd prefer to drop by sooner than that if it's okay. I already have a dinner engagement. Give me an hour to wrap this up, and I'll be there—a little before that if I can do it."

"That's better for me," Judy said. "I have to get home before dark to make sure all the chores have been done. I don't do them all myself anymore, but I still need to make sure they're done the way they ought to be done."

"Do you know how to find my aunt's house?" I asked.

"Benchley does. I'll make sure she gives me directions."

"Okay," I turned and started to leave. Then I stopped. "When I was here this morning, Beth Varner seemed to indicate Franklin's afternoon wasn't a busy one. Does that mean no one was scheduled to meet with him?"

"Franklin Everett had an appointment with someone, but she canceled at the last minute. His associates were out of the office today—one of them is in court in San Jose, and the other is on vacation. Obviously, they didn't have any appointments. Isn't that right, Beth?" I turned to see Franklin's receptionist enter the room. Her eyes were red-rimmed, and her caramel-colored cheeks were streaked with tears. I waited to hear her response to Officer Benchley's question.

"The Laughton woman, who's the sweetest little thing—Connie Laughton, was the only one on his calendar today besides Lily. I checked. She'll be so upset." Something about the name struck a chord—as if I'd heard it somewhere before. I tried to recall where. When no answer came speedily, I gave up.

"I don't suppose there are surveillance cameras in place, are there?" Austin asked.

"No," Beth responded. "There's a traffic camera set up at the cross-street. Franklin always joked that no one was going to break in here with that camera watching them." Austin sent a glance Dahlia's way. She bobbed her head noncommittally.

"Hey, it's worth a try," he said as she pulled off her latex gloves and grabbed a phone out of her jacket pocket.

"Why not?" Dahlia asked as she placed a call.

"Who would do this to him?" Beth sobbed. Tears had begun to run down her cheeks again. "He was such a kind-hearted man. His wife is devastated as you can imagine. It's the worst news I've ever had to give anyone."

"I'm sure it was better for Franklin's family to hear it from you than from the police or media. Aunt Lettie liked him very much even though he hadn't always been her lawyer," I said. "I wish I'd had a chance to get to know him better."

Given the misery on Beth's face, the words rang empty as I spoke them. She'd nodded at me, but with a hint of wariness in her expression as if she hadn't made up her mind about me yet. Someone from the county coroner's office wheeled in a cart, and we stepped out of the way. A body bag was lying on it. That was it! I was ready to go.

"We should get out of here, so you can finish your work." Dahlia, who was still on the phone, waved at us. Officer Benchley turned her back on us without saying a word.

When we got outside onto the porch, I sucked in great gulps of fresh air. I felt dirty, either because of the horrific scene or because of the repeated attempts to impute the horror to me. Perhaps, it was a layer of guilt that had settled over me wondering if by coming home I had provoked the crime spree.

"Judy, have you heard Connie Laughton's name before? It sounds familiar to me, but I can't place her," I asked as we walked to the car.

"No, I don't believe I have. There aren't any Laughtons in Calistoga. Maybe in Napa, though, since it's a much larger city. Could you have met someone by that name there? Or maybe it was someone from high school."

"I don't know," I said as we climbed into Judy's truck. She'd insisted on driving since she was more familiar with the route to Franklin's office than Austin or me.

"Now that I think about it, Lettie may have mentioned someone by the name of Laughton—not recently though—and I don't believe it was anyone local." Judy shrugged and turned on the engine. "It must not have been anyone too important, or we'd remember, right?"

"Right now, I'm lucky to remember my own name. Maybe it'll come back to me." Austin reached out and gave my hand a squeeze. Judy noticed and gave me a wink as she pulled out of the lot. I bent down a little to spot the camera as we went through the intersection. It wasn't mounted overhead, but off to one side.

"I've been through this intersection several times and didn't notice the camera until now. It obviously wasn't a deterrent to Franklin's killer. Maybe the rat tore out of here fast enough to trigger the camera."

"It's more likely a red-light than a speeding camera given how big it is. The same principle applies, though. Anyone in a big hurry to get away, might not have cared whether the light had changed or not. That's why I thought Dahlia ought to check it out. Don't get your hopes up," Austin added.

9

Unlucky in Love

I CHECKED THE time when we arrived back at Aunt Lettie's home. It hadn't taken us long, but if Dahlia Ahern could get here in the next hour or so, it would be a miracle. Maybe she could leave Benchley in charge—Officer Benchley appeared as if she was competent enough to do that. The evidence specialists from the Sheriff's Department's Investigation Bureau could probably do their job without Deputy Ahern or anyone else hovering over them.

Judy drove up to the gate at the entrance to the property and punched in the code on a keypad.

How many people, besides Judy, have the code? I wondered. I tried to remember where Aunt Lettie kept the instructions for how to change it. Maybe on her laptop. Before the gate was completely open, Jesse was there. He waved us down.

"Did that woman catch up with you?" he asked when Judy rolled down her window.

"What woman? We just left Deputy Ahern. She didn't get here ahead of us, did she?"

"Uh, no deputies—other than him." Jesse glanced at Austin, and then paused as he spotted Austin's hand resting next to mine—almost on my lap. Jesse's eyes were a little darker when he made eye contact with me a moment later. As he leaned in the window, his entire face was cast in shadow. There were circles under his eyes and hollows in his cheeks I hadn't seen earlier. Life had taken a toll on Jesse that was beyond what age alone could have done. "This one was young. She said she needed to speak to Lily about Lettie and wanted me to let her in so she could wait up at the house. I told her you haven't even moved in yet, Lily, and she should call you or come by again in a couple of days once you get settled."

"Did you give her Aunt Lettie's phone number?" I asked.

"No. I figured she already had it since she didn't ask for it."

"Was it Carol Matheson?" Judy asked.

"It could have been her. I've never spoken to her or seen her up close though. This woman had brown eyes and brown hair that stopped about here." Jesse used his hand to demonstrate that the woman's hair was chin-length.

"The hair and eyes sound about right," Judy said.

"She didn't leave a name?" I asked.

"No. I guess I should have asked."

"Maybe she didn't think she needed to do that. After we talked a while ago, I called Carol and left a message that we had questions for her. She could have thought that meant we were expecting her."

"Well, I can only handle one more visitor tonight.

Thanks for not letting anyone in without checking with me first." That made Jesse smile. "Deputy Ahern will call me, and I'll buzz her in from the house, so she shouldn't have to bother you."

"It's no bother. I've got your back!" Jesse gave me a thumbs up and smacked Judy's door a couple times as he backed up to let us pass.

"If it was the nurse, Carol, responding to your call, why didn't she just say that? You know, 'tell Judy I dropped by' or something like that? Or why hasn't she called you?" I asked.

"I don't know. I hope I didn't imply that I thought she was responsible for Lettie's death somehow. If she's as stressed out about all this as I am, she could be a little scatterbrained. I'm at my limit, too, when it comes to talking to people about this mess tonight. Franklin Everett's battered body was one of the worst things I've ever seen. How do you cops do it?" Judy asked as she drove up the hill to the house.

"It's not easy. You never get completely used to it. It's harder when it's someone you know," Austin replied, his voice grew quieter when he uttered those last few words. "You should have surveillance cameras installed on those gates—that way you can get a visual of anyone asking to be admitted onto the property before you buzz them in from the house. If they were already installed, we'd have a tape to look at. That would be better than wondering who Jesse spoke to earlier. I can't believe he didn't get a name."

"He's not trained in security, like you, Austin. I think he's trying to be conscientious by hanging around the gate. Under normal circumstances, our mystery guest would have stopped, buzzed to get in, and when no one answered, left. We wouldn't have even known we had a visitor."

"Cameras would fix that, too."

"I hear you. I'll look into it."

"Let me do that. I can find someone who'll do it right."

"That would be great!" I reached out and patted Austin's hand.

"I've got your back, too!" Austin gave me two thumbs up.

"Hey, be kind. Jesse's trying to be helpful."

"Helpful like a wolf on the prowl," Judy muttered as she pulled into the large driveway in front of Aunt Lettie's house.

"My thoughts exactly!" Austin added as Judy parked and shut off the engine. I was too tired to argue with them. Besides, they were probably right, although, if he was a wolf, Jesse struck me as a sad, lonely one. Once Austin hopped out of Judy's truck, I followed still wondering about our visitor.

"Judy, if you leave her number for me, I'll call Carol tomorrow. You've already done more than your share. I have several calls to make in the morning including touching base with the funeral home about burial arrangements for Aunt Lettie. Did the coroner tell you how much longer it'll be before she releases Aunt Lettie to us?"

"When I spoke to her yesterday, she said another day or two. If you call her in the morning, she can give you a better idea than I can. Call her first and then Sam Clementson, the funeral director. He'll take it from there. Lettie left all the instructions with him about how she wanted to be buried—who to invite, what music to play, who to offer a benediction, along with strict orders to keep the burial ceremony brief." I could hear Marlowe yipping at us from inside as I walked up the porch steps. As soon as I opened the door, I scooped him up.

"Okay. I hope we can keep the investigation into Aunt Lettie's death brief, too. I want to know the truth. Even if someone killed her, finding out who did it and why won't bring her back, will it?" I snuggled Marlowe as we stood in the foyer. Judy shut the door. "I keep expecting to hear her walking around upstairs, talking to herself, or clanking pots in the kitchen. She filled this house with her spirit while she was alive. It feels so empty even with the three of us and Marlowe here. The B&B may not be a bad idea."

"You don't have to make a decision about the B&B right now with so much going on. No matter what else we do, we'll celebrate Lettie's life. Lettie was emphatic that she wanted us to have a small funeral and a big party. She has that all planned too with wine, food, and music during an open house at the Winery. I think you should wait a little while. Treat it like a memorial service and hold it later."

"I agree. Especially now that there will have to be another funeral so soon. It won't be much of a party, either, with Franklin's killer still on the loose and Aunt Lettie's too, if it turns out she was also murdered," I added.

"True. Bringing the killings to a stop and getting justice for Lettie and Franklin is reason enough to go on now even if it doesn't bring them back." Judy showed the first real signs of anger I'd seen from the sturdy, stoic eightysomething woman.

"At least we're not in this alone. Dahlia strikes me as dogged and determined. Officer Benchley is too, although I hope she casts her suspicions elsewhere, fast, and quits picking on me. Austin and his boss, Rikki Havens, are also working on this. One of them, or one of us, is bound to come up with something that can put a stop to it soon. I'm really happy about not having to attend a third funeral—my own, thanks to Austin." He put an arm around me and gave me a kiss on the forehead.

"Me, too. Let's have a toast to your Aunt Lettie. You brought up a bottle of wine from the cellar, why don't I open it and pour us a glass while we wait for Dahlia to get here?"

"I could use a drink. Follow me." Judy took off again. She darted down the hall and then into the dining room. Marlowe sped after her. I took off my spiky heels and massaged my sore feet.

"I can do that for you," Austin whispered, as a spark of something almost as tangible as static electricity passed between us. "I'm pretty good at it, too."

"I'll bet you are. Speaking of wolves on the prowl, you've probably had plenty of opportunities to practice your technique." My cynicism countered the effects of the spark. I pushed past Austin, carrying my shoes. He was wearing one of those enticing smiles—not a leer, but open and engaging. Despite my protestations, I was tempted to take him up on his offer. I never dreamed I'd be wearing the shoes all day. Besides, how much trouble could we get into with Judy here as our chaperone?

"Not as much as you seem to believe," Austin added.

"What?" I asked. It sounded almost as if he'd responded to the question I'd just asked myself. I hadn't spoken it
out loud, had I?

"So many bad guys, so little time. I haven't had that
much opportunity to practice my technique," he replied
still speaking in a whisper. I shook my head, not believing
him for a minute as we entered the dining room.

"I have no doubt you're a busy man, Marshal." Judy
already had wine glasses and a corkscrew out on the
granite counter. The beautiful painting Aunt Lettie had left
for Judy, caught my eye as Austin and I passed by on our
way into the butler's pantry.

"Austin offered to pour the wine. I'll bet he knows his
way around a cork."

"I'll bet he does, too," Judy added, winking at me.
Austin smirked. When the two of us ogled him in an
exaggerated fashion, his smirk faded.

"Let's take him up on the offer," I added. Then Austin
shook his head and grinned.

"Wine for three, coming right up! How much trouble
can we get into with a sheriff's deputy on her way?" My
mouth dropped open as I wondered once again if I'd
uttered instead of just thinking almost the same words
moments ago. I wasn't sure which was worse—
accidentally speaking my thoughts aloud without realizing
it, or the prospect that the hunky, good-natured lawman
could read my mind. A surge of embarrassment rushed
through me as I considered the mind reading option, even
though I knew it was ridiculous. Still, no way was I willing
to share my thoughts with him as my feigned ogling
turned into the real deal. Time to change the subject.

"Why don't we get your Ruth Westphal packed up properly, so you can take it home with you after Dahlia leaves?"

"I'd love to do that. It won't take much—maybe wrap it in some brown paper and tie it up with string. That way, when I get home, I won't have to do anything except rip off the paper and hang it. I have a spot already picked out where the lighting's perfect. Every time I see it, I'll remember all the wonderful times we had together." Judy was getting teary again, and so was I.

"Come on. We'll get it ready for you, and you can fill me in about how you've organized the stuff in here. That way I can get the other gifts to the people Aunt Lettie chose to receive them soon."

"Why wait? Let's do it now."

We worked steadily at the task of packing Lettie's lovely possessions. Judy, in her incredibly thoughtful way, had not only found Aunt Lettie's supplies but had bought more to speed the task along. Each of Aunt Lettie's gifts brought back memories for me. For Judy, too, I soon found out. Austin listened as we spoke, asking a question here and there. Judy stopped what she was doing and held out her empty wine glass for a refill.

"What about you, Austin? Do you have an aunt Lettie somewhere?" Austin had been sitting across from me at the dining table. He stood and poured more of the wonderful deep red cab into Judy's glass.

"No. I already told Lily that I spent most of my childhood shuttling back and forth between my parents and my grandparents. My parents moved constantly, so the closest place I have to a home is Redding where my grandparents lived. My granddad loved the outdoors, and I spent lots of time hunting and fishing with him. He had a wonderful, dry sense of humor, and loved to pull pranks on my grandma. She was a very patient woman. As he grew older, he'd pull the same stunts on her repeatedly, and she always acted as if she'd fallen for it again. Their relationship has probably kept me from becoming completely cynical about love and marriage." Austin shrugged. "As a cop, seeing what some people do to each other in the name of love, I wish they were still around to offset my skepticism."

"Lettie and I always considered love a crapshoot. I got lucky; she didn't. Not that there weren't plenty of men interested in her over the years."

"Romantically?" I asked.

"Don't act so surprised."

"She always seemed to have plenty of men friends, but none of them ever appeared to be suitors," I said.

"By the time you moved in with her, she'd learned to quickly give the men in her life the news that her heart was taken." My head popped up from where I was trying to tape a package and bolloxed the job.

"What does that mean?" I asked.

Austin leaned in from where he'd sat down at the table. He reached out and held down the edge of the paper so I could undo the tape that had stuck together when I took my eyes off the task.

"When I said she was unlucky, I didn't mean Lettie never fell in love." Judy paused and got a faraway look in her eye. "Not every love story has a happy ending."

10

Lucky at Cards

"LETTIE WAS A girl still—sixteen—when she fell for James Sanders. A year later, they were engaged, but he was drafted during the Korean conflict. He left home and never came back. Apparently, Lettie lost it for a time. Her family shipped her off up north hoping she'd recover."

"That must have worked," I said.

"Not as far as her family members in Alabama were concerned. Lettie tried to find solace in religion. She became involved with a group of nuns who were doing outreach with the poor. Your aunt toyed with the idea of converting to Catholicism, but it was their political activism that brought her out of the pit of grief she'd fallen into."

"No wonder they labeled her a black sheep," I said as I finally got the package taped properly.

"Well, she was already suspect before she left home. They considered her inability to free herself from her grief after James Sanders was killed a moral failing, and her involvement in the Catholic Peace and Justice movement didn't redeem her. What really earned her the black sheep label was that she joined the Civil Rights movement in the late fifties. Lettie returned home to the south, but not the way they planned for her to do it."

"I sort of knew all of this, but I never put it all together well enough to understand how she'd alienated herself from her family. She also told me they thought she'd sold her soul to the devil when she won this place in a card game. Is it true that's what happened?"

"Her life was a little like that old saying: 'lucky at cards, unlucky at love.' Yes, she won the property in a card game. It wasn't much of a prize. Lettie worked her butt off for twenty years before her efforts bore fruit. In this case, I mean that literally, given how productive the vines became thanks to her determination and effort. You already know that the winery and the success she's had with it is an even more recent development."

"Aunt Lettie always told me fortune smiled on her. She claimed she was in the right place at the right time when she settled down here. I knew the story about winning this place in a card game wasn't the whole story. Aunt Lettie also mentioned that an aunt had left her 'encouragement money' just when she needed it. When my mother made snide comments about the fact that Aunt Lettie's hands were calloused, and she dressed like a man, I found it fascinating."

"Lettie was a far stretch from the image of the Southern Belle in *Gone with the Wind,* that's for sure. It's also true the small inheritance Lettie received kept her going. I believe that's why it was so important for her to leave you a legacy. It's more about the encouragement than the money." Her eyes were shiny with tears, again. I stopped what I was doing to give her a hug. Then, picked up my glass and gave hers a clink.

"To our wonderful, cherished friend," I said.

"A woman I wish I'd met," Austin said as he raised his glass, too.

"The biggest stroke of luck Lettie had was the fact that land and property prices around here took off. She was smart about leveraging the land to make improvements that made it all worth more. She expanded her holdings, too. In '62, her entire stake here—house, land, and everything—was probably worth about fifty thousand dollars. I'm sure Franklin told you it's worth a staggering amount now. Most of that's tied up, so its value is more in assets than in cash."

"Staggering is right. When I came to live with her when I was twelve, Aunt Lettie spent so much time with me, I never really thought of her as a businesswoman. If I take a minute to reflect, I can recall how much time she spent going over accounts and doing paperwork. She was often on the phone taking care of an issue about the vineyards or the winery, or going to meetings, and community affairs. She made it appear easy. In my kid-centered way back then, she was more like a delightful playmate than a working woman. I always felt as if I was her priority."

"You came along at exactly the right time. That was another stroke of luck for Lettie. The business she created had become so big and complex it was no longer a one-woman operation. I'd never seen her happier than she was once you moved in. Lettie was in her sixties then, and not planning to retire, but she was ready to step back a little and let others take the lead on day-to-day operations. You gave her a new purpose—a chance to focus on family. You became her most important project.

"Growing up with Aunt Lettie to guide me was the best thing that ever happened to me," I said. "How anyone could hold a grudge against her is impossible to imagine."

"Success has its drawbacks. A bigger business means more money and more people who want a cut. That can spell bigger trouble, too, more often than you know." Austin said that as if he knew it all too well. Another unhappy consequence of tracking down bad guys for a living, I suppose.

"Last one," I said a couple of minutes later. So far, we'd packed all the gifts in a way that made it possible for me to carry them to the people Lettie cared so much about, or so they could pick them up if they preferred. There was a lovely vintage silver tea service left. This gift had to be mailed. The recipient surprised me just a little.

"This is a name I hadn't heard Lettie mention in years. I wasn't sure Emma was still alive or that she and Lettie were still in touch."

"Her sister was the only family member Lettie ever really cared about other than you. She probably didn't tell you that Emma's the person who took her in after James was killed. Emma had left Alabama a couple of years before when she got married. She managed to stay on speaking terms with the rest of the clan, although Emma's life wasn't any more conventional than Lettie's. She was more inclined to keep to herself than Lettie who antagonized everyone when she returned 'home' filled with righteous indignation about her families' politics."

"The bequest is to Emma Morgan. That's her maiden name. I'm sure there was a different last name for her in Aunt Lettie's family Bible."

"Lettie could have recorded Emma's married name as well as her maiden name. When I said Emma's life wasn't conventional, in part what I meant by that, is that she divorced her husband a couple of years after Lettie returned to Alabama. If it hadn't been for Lettie's new-found social activism, Emma's divorce would probably have been a bigger family scandal than it was. Emma had a toddler at the time. After her divorce, Emma got a job and became a working woman like Lettie. Because Lettie created such a stink, Emma was able to avoid attention."

"I don't remember any mention of a child, but it's been years since I saw her Bible. I wonder where it is." *Is that where I'd run into the Laughton name?* I wondered.

"Emma's still alive, obviously, but her daughter, Ann, died a few years ago. She was in her fifties. I'm sure Lettie added that to the information she tracked in the family Bible. Lettie was torn up about it—said it's rough when a mother outlives her child. Lettie tried to get Emma to visit her here in California. I don't know how Ann died, but it must have been hard on Emma."

"I'm sure it was. Franklin said Lettie had set up a trust fund several years ago for a grandniece—outside the context of the Will. I'm not sure if he said her name was Ann. In fact, I can't remember now if he mentioned a name at all."

"If it was Lettie's grandniece, it would have been a gift

to Emma's granddaughter, not her daughter, Ann. Emma's granddaughter could also have been named Ann if she was given her mother's name. That's not too unusual. If you find the Bible, Lettie's records ought to clear up the confusion. It must be on the bookshelf in her room or in her closet. When Lettie redid the den and turned it into more of a reading room for B&B guests to use, she moved her personal items upstairs."

"Does Emma know Lettie's dead?"

"I doubt it. I called Lettie's local friends. Franklin may have notified Emma or may have been in the process of doing it in fulfillment of the terms of the Will. Lily, why don't you call before you send her the tea set? She shouldn't have to find out about her sister's death through the Morgan family grapevine. Despite their great disappointment at the paltry sum Lettie left them, your mother sounds like a woman who'll make sure the word gets out." I nodded in agreement. Calling Emma was the right thing to do, even though I dreaded being the bearer of bad news.

Before I could respond, the doorbell rang. Deputy Sheriff Dahlia Ahern had arrived. Judy invited her to have a seat in the parlor.

"Officer Benchley told me to prepare to be impressed. This place is huge. Gorgeous, too."

"Thank you," I said. "I haven't settled in yet, so I'm limited in what I can offer you as your hostess. Judy brought us cookies and milk. I'd be happy to share them with you. Or I can pour you a glass of the Calla Lily Cabernet we've been drinking if you prefer."

"It's a tough choice, Dahlia," Austin said. "You don't want to miss out on the cookies." He'd obviously gone back into the kitchen to help himself since he was holding another of the soft chunky chocolate chip cookies Judy had baked.

"I didn't think I could eat a thing tonight after having spent so much time at that crime scene. You've changed my mind. I'll take that cookie, please." She reached out for it. Austin pulled his arm back a little.

"I'll get you one. Do you want milk too?" Austin asked.

"Technically, I'm still on duty, so I should probably have a glass of milk. It's nearing the end of a long, hard day and I can't think of anything better than a chocolate chip cookie and a good glass of Cab. Oh, what the heck, I'll take the wine."

"You get the cookie, and I'll pour Dahlia's wine." I was almost sorry I'd tried to play hostess given the delay this was causing in getting to the point of Dahlia's visit. Then I heard Lettie's voice as clear as if she was standing there in front of me.

"Southern hospitality is one of the few redeeming features of my upbringing. A kind and welcoming spirit never hurts—in fact, it's uplifting. Redemptive even."

As she'd often done, Aunt Lettie smiled with an inner radiance as she spoke those words. Entertaining brought her such joy—joy that I don't feel. Socializing had become all about work for me. In Hollywood, it was about seeing and being seen rather than being with people who mattered to you. I poured wine into a crystal goblet for Dahlia.

"To you!" I said raising the glass in tribute to Aunt Lettie as I carried the deep ruby elixir to Dahlia.

"Thank you, Lily." Dahlia took a sip. "Wow!"

"Wait until you taste these," Austin said handing Dahlia a plate of cookies.

"Double wow!"

"It's one of Lily's aunt's recipes. Great, huh?"

"You've got that right, cowboy." Dahlia winked at Austin. I tried not to roll my eyes, wondering once again what had gone on between these two and how long ago. Thankfully, Judy was getting anxious and prodded Dahlia the way I wanted to do.

"I've got to get home soon, so if you have questions for me, you need to ask them, Deputy." Dahlia nodded, her mouth too full to speak. She closed her eyes for a second, savoring the chocolaty flavor and chewy texture of the cookie. Crunchy, too, since Judy had tossed in toasted pecans as Lettie liked to do at times. The social amenities out of the way and that cookie gone, Dahlia got down to business, speaking to me first.

"According to Beth Varner, you've come into quite a fortune. She also claims your relatives weren't exactly happy for you. Did they ever threaten your aunt or her lawyer?"

"Yes, yes, and no." Dahlia blinked. "Yes, my inheritance is substantial. And yes, it's also true my parents and half-siblings weren't thrilled. My stepfather appeared to be the most obviously disgruntled family member. I didn't know it beforehand, but Lettie had loaned them money— debt that she forgave in her Will. Given her generosity while she was alive, I suppose Eddie could have expected they'd cash in big when she died. If he and his children were willing to be more patient, Lettie's bequest to them could have amounted to much more than the one hundred fifty thousand dollars they walked away with today." Dahlia almost choked at the number I rattled off as she ate a ginger crisp cookie that Austin had put on the plate he'd brought her. "No threats as far as I know. Most of her life, they wanted little to do with Lettie or me."

"Except using her as a piggy bank given that she'd loaned them money." I nodded. Dahlia's statement hit the nail on the head. "Okay, so Dad's got a greedy streak. That's a possible motive. It sounds like they might have money problems. Maybe they hoped if they broke open the piggy bank, they'd get the money they needed to make their problems go away." She sipped her wine, and then spoke to Judy.

"That might be a reason to kill Letitia Morgan if you're right and she was murdered. Officer Benchley says you're the one who found Lettie and you suspected foul play. By the way the police report reads, you didn't convince Barb; so convince me, okay?"

I couldn't stop from rolling my eyes this time. Dahlia missed it, but Austin caught it and looked down at his lap to hide the smile my behavior evoked. Judy recounted the story she'd already told us. Dahlia was following along without much interest until Judy brought up the issue of the drugs. That got through to Dahlia and triggered her wary cop side.

"When I track down Marcia Devers at the coroner's office to ask for the details about Franklin Everett's death, I'll make sure she also lets me know what she learns when Lettie's test results get back. I'll take those bits of china off your hands while I'm here. It's too bad the authorities didn't collect them while they were at the scene, but if you didn't know about the sedative issue until later, there was no reason for Benchley to do it."

"My parents weren't anywhere near here at the time, so I doubt you can charge them with much more than greed and stupidity," I offered.

"That's probably true. I'll do a little checking to make sure daddy dearest didn't make an earlier trip to California to visit your aunt. If he did, maybe he also hired the gunmen to go after you while he was out here. Did Franklin Everett tell you who stands to get all the goodies if something happens to you, Lily?"

"There weren't any provisions written into my aunt's will about that. I hate to believe my parents are drooling over the prospect that if I die, my mother or half-siblings are in line to inherit Lettie's property. There's no love lost between us, but it never entered my mind they disliked me enough to kill me for my inheritance. They didn't ask Beth such a question, did they?"

"No. She said your mother did ask an odd question about whether Lettie had any children of her own."

"That is odd. Lettie left a valuable vintage silver tea set to her sister, and at some point, she directed Franklin to set up a trust fund for a niece—a grandniece most likely since Judy just told me her sister's daughter is dead."

"Sorry, I'm lost. I need you to draw me a picture, I'm afraid. I never can get all the family ties straight. What I gather, though, is that if you died, her sister would be first in line as Lettie's closest living relative. Her niece would have been next, except she's dead, so that leaves a grand-niece as next in line, right?"

"Yes, since I'm not married and have no children, Lettie's sister and her offspring are next in line. My mother would be in the running, but she wouldn't be first. Her husband and kids would have even less claim to Lettie's assets."

"Are Lily's relatives still in town?" Austin asked.

"Yes. I'm checking on their whereabouts and what they did after they took their checks and left Franklin Everett's office. I was doing that in a routine way, but now that Lily's told us how disappointed Eddie Callahan was about the terms of the Will, I'll take a closer look. If he doubled back, tried to persuade Franklin to come up with more money, and couldn't get him to do it, maybe that triggered the beating that killed Lettie's lawyer. I've asked for the camera data as you suggested, Austin. It's a longshot given that it's unlikely the killer was stupid enough to commit a traffic violation on their way to or from a murderous assault on Franklin. Barb Benchley also made a good point that the killer didn't even have to come or go that way. There's plenty of parking along the street and behind the building."

"I could see the killer arriving that way," I said. "Parking on the street and walking to the law office wouldn't have drawn much attention. Walking back to the car, covered in blood after bashing Franklin Everett's brains in, might have raised a few eyebrows, though, don't you think?"

"Thanks for creating such a vivid picture of events." Dahlia set her wine down. "I didn't say that's what happened, just that it was possible for the killer to have arrived and departed on foot. Maybe the killer went in dressed as you were this morning, Lily. I hear you wore a tailor-made top coat over the stunning dress you still have on. The ensemble left an indelible impression on Beth. That's one reason she was so sure the expensive pair of sunglasses found on Franklin's desk was yours."

"How fortunate that I was able to make a fashion statement even under such ghoulish circumstances—the reading of a dead woman's Last Will and Testament, followed by the bloodthirsty murder of her lawyer." I tapped my foot in distress about the pointless references to me while Franklin's killer roamed free.

"My point was that Franklin's killer could have worn an overcoat like you did, taken it off, done the deed, and then put it back on to cover the gore. No one would have noticed much as the person walked away," Dahlia said.

"Here's what I regard as a more relevant question regardless of how the killer arrived or was dressed. If Franklin was there alone while Beth ran her errands, would they have left the door unlocked?"

"Beth swears she locked it when she left but found it unlocked when she returned. If Franklin had a visitor, he must have let the person in. It wouldn't have been the first time Franklin left the door unlocked after walking a person out at the end of a meeting."

"Okay, so theoretically it's possible Franklin had more than one visitor if he left the door unlocked. A perfect stranger who entered the law office in broad daylight for some unknown reason. Not a robbery since, as I recall, there were pricey items, like a laptop, in plain view on the receptionist's desk. I think it's far more likely Franklin let someone in—someone he knew who killed him, and then ran out without locking the door.'"

"That would be my guess, too. We'll see what the coroner's report finds, but her initial investigation suggests he didn't put up a struggle or make any effort to block the first blow, so he must have been caught by surprise. That would have been easier to do if he was familiar with his visitor and the person had never given him a reason to be on his guard."

"Or who appeared to be harmless," Austin added.

"Like a willowy, attractive young woman you mean?" Dahlia was making a point with Austin that I didn't get, but he did.

"Yes, Dahlia, if that's the description Beth Varner gave you of the client who had an appointment with Franklin and then canceled it. Maybe she changed her mind and showed up anyway."

"I've got an interview set up with Connie Laughton for tomorrow morning. Beth described her as cute, with brown hair and brown eyes—petite, shy, and soft-spoken—I made up the willowy attractive bit. I'll let you know more after I meet with her." I wasn't sure what was going on with that exchange between Dahlia and Austin, but it hadn't revealed anything helpful.

"Okay, so petite, shy, and soft-spoken are traits that fit the 'harmless' profile. Given Franklin's congenial demeanor, I doubt he'd find anyone threatening before it was too late—male or female. What did the harmless visitor who caught him by surprise use to kill him? Did you find a murder weapon?"

"Yes, we did. It's an eight-inch long, flat edge, rigid metal file with an orange loop handle at one end made by a company called Bahco. It's a tool used in lots of vine-yards and by gardeners. We won't know for sure until the coroner's done her work, but I'm fairly certain the killer used it like a knife despite the fact the edge is flat and not pointy." Dahlia made a series of stabbing motions as if she was reenacting the classic shower scene from Psycho. "Once his head was down, he was an easy target for his killer's rage."

"You're not talking about a sharpening tool, are you?" I asked.

"Barb called it something like that. Don't tell me you left more than your sunglasses in Franklin's office?"

"We're not back to that again, are we? Thank good-ness I was in the company of a Deputy U.S. Marshal at the time my aunt's lawyer was slaughtered." This was getting old. I paused to get myself under control. "I don't own one, but Aunt Lettie and most of her friends have used them for years to sharpen their gardening tools. That's Aunt Lettie's brand."

"Would you mind showing me where she keeps it?" Dahlia asked, draining her wine glass as if she was ready to go.

"I can try. I haven't even moved in yet, and my aunt changed lots of things during a flurry of recent renova-tions. She used to keep it in a tool shed near her greenhouse. I don't believe it's locked, so if you want to check, knock yourself out."

"I'll show you to the shed," Judy offered. "I've been in there more recently than Lily. Lettie kept it hanging on a hook—let's go see if it's still there. Then, I'd like to get in my truck and go home if you don't have more questions.

You can follow me home and check my tools, too, if you want. I've got one of them, too." Judy was clearly ready to go, but she paused and spoke again.

"There is one more person we should call attention to before I take you to the shed. We had an interesting conversation before you arrived about Alexander Davidson. He's another person with whom Franklin might have felt at ease until the conversation took an unexpected turn."

"Judy's making an excellent point. I'm a little surprised Alexander Davidson's name hasn't already come up. Didn't Beth tell you he was as upset as my stepfather after Franklin finished his reading of the Will?"

"She said he was confused, not upset." Dahlia's brow furrowed as she considered the latest twist we'd introduced.

"Well, I'll go on record saying he was upset. He was almost accusatory when he questioned Franklin about the Will—as if Franklin Everett had not only let him down but also betrayed him. Maybe he went back to have it out with Franklin, flew into a rage, and lost control."

"Why would he care that much whether it's you or your aunt sitting on the board?" Dahlia asked.

I could have offered her a bunch of the reasons we'd kicked around earlier, but at this point, we had nothing to offer her except speculation. I was exhausted. Creeped out, too, by Dahlia's ghastly retelling of the way Franklin had died. We had no way to connect Alexander Davidson or anyone else at the Calla Lily Vineyards and Winery to wine fraud so we wouldn't get far by bringing that up either.

"I was hoping Beth could tell you more about it. Franklin may have discussed it with her or with Lettie in front of Beth. If my experience today wasn't an unusual one, it appears his receptionist doubles as a secretary at meetings. Maybe you should have another conversation with her tomorrow when she's not in a state of shock."

"I'll put it on the list," Dahlia said. She suddenly sounded as worn out as I felt. "I'll also go directly to the source and ask Alexander Davidson why he was so taken aback by the news you're going to be taking Lettie's place on the board at the Calla Lily Winery." She stood up and spoke to Judy.

"Let's go see if our murder weapon could have come from Lettie's shed. I've got a sneaking suspicion we won't find one in there. Maybe whoever tried to kill Lily decided having her sent to prison for murder was almost as good as killing her."

"Lucky me! If you're right, my odds of living through this just went way up. By the clumsy way in which I've been set up so far, I'm not too worried about going to the slammer. I would like to get to the bottom of this soon, though."

"I already suggested you cool it—don't push your luck! If I were you, I'd focus on beefing up security around here. If Lettie's sharpening tool was used to murder Franklin Everett, how did it get from the tool shed?"

"The killer must have been here on the property at some point," Judy mumbled.

"Great! That narrows it down to a cast of thousands—friends, associates, or employees—including the host of contractors Aunt Lettie hired to renovate the place. And let's not forget about the workers who are brought in to work in the fields."

"Surely, they don't all have the run of the place, do they?" Dahlia asked.

"I wish I could say that wasn't true. My aunt was a trusting soul. I'm sure she felt safe with the gates at the entrance. Austin's already made it clear our security could be better."

"Then, I'll say goodnight and leave you in the capable hands of Deputy U.S. Marshal Austin Jennings." My whole body stiffened. If Dahlia winked or smirked again, I might just take a chance on going to jail by smacking her one. Maybe the routine was getting old for her too now. She turned to Judy and spoke in a weary, deadly serious tone.

"Let's go see what new mysteries await us in Letitia Morgan's tool shed." Judy picked up the painting we'd wrapped for her as she replied.

"As long as it's not another dead body, I can cope."

11

A Change of Luck

"FINALLY, WE'RE ALONE!" Austin said when the door closed behind Judy and Dahlia. He swept me into his arms. "Where were we before we were so rudely interrupted?" The kiss that followed took my breath away.

I took a half-step back, coming up for air, and trying to right myself in a world that was upside down. Events from the past twenty-four hours flashed through my mind like a horror movie being run on "fast forward." It would be easy to lose myself in Austin's embrace—and his very capable hands as Dahlia had felt the need to point out.

"Rudely interrupted by a bloodthirsty murder you mean? Or by one of my aunt's oldest friends bringing us the news that someone may have killed the woman who was more a mother than an aunt to me?" I leaned in and put my head on his chest. "This is easily the worst day of my life. That's saying something, too, after nearly being blown away in a hail of bullets last night.

"I'm trying to make it all better," Austin said. "Where does it hurt? Here?" He asked, kissing my cheek. "How about here?" Then he kissed me a little lower, working his way down to my neck.

"That's definitely better," I said, succumbing once again to the comfort and pleasure I found in his touch. When he reached up and pulled the hairpins from my chignon, my hair tumbled freely down my back. I was on the verge of tumbling, too, toward a point of no return.

Judy's words came back to me about love being a crap-shoot. In my condition, I was in no shape to roll the dice on love. Besides, it was too early in the game to do that. I'm old enough to know that attraction may be instanta-neous. Love and all the hefty issues that go with it—trust, commitment, compromise, and sacrifice—take more time to develop.

My breakup with Tony hadn't been so long ago that I'd forgotten the pain involved when we decided to go our separate ways. That was true even though by then it was obvious to both of us we'd lost at love. At this point, I'm not even sure it was ever about love. I was grateful to Tony because he'd done so much for me. Gratitude felt a lot like love. I was scared too about spending my life alone as I approached thirty without having met my soulmate.

"This is moving too fast for me, Austin. My life is spinning out of control. I wasn't prepared for any of this when I drove up here yesterday. Not only being caught up in all the murder and mayhem but meeting an incredible man, I...I've been knocked off balance." Austin beamed.

"Me, too. You threw the first punch, remember? I don't want to waste a minute of the time we have together. On the other hand, there's no rush since I'm never letting you go." He pulled me to him and rested his chin against my head, stroking my hair. "You promised to buy me dinner, remember?"

"That's true, and I'd never break a promise to a Deputy U.S. Marshal." The kiss that followed didn't take long to drag us back toward the edge of a cliff. Then Dahlia's smirking face loomed up between us. "You know Dahlia better than I do. Maybe over dinner, you can help me read between the lines. Does she have any idea about what's going on or not?"

"I don't know her as well as you think I do—not in the way you think I do, anyway. Dahlia's a good investigator. Dahlia, Rikki, and I have known each other for years. We've worked cases together, too. I told you my grandparents are the reason I haven't given up on love. Unlucky at love is an understatement when it comes to me."

"I find that impossible to believe. Then again, I've told you about Tony, and you've met Jesse. My track record is short and sad, so what do I know?"

"Your luck can't be worse than mine unless it turns out Tony, the dim-witted agent who cheated on you, also hired the hitmen we have in custody. Although, from Rikki's latest update about Tony, the trail doesn't seem to lead back to him. Probably the worst luck I ever had was to fall for a woman who disappeared a few weeks into our relationship with my brand-new truck. When I dug into her past, it turned out she was wanted in half a dozen states. The only satisfying part of the entire experience was handing her over to the FBI so she could pay for her crimes."

"Will you lend me your badge? I'd like to give Tony a good scare even if he's not the one who paid to have me killed." Austin laughed.

"He deserves it, but he's already facing a life sentence without you." Austin shook his head. "Dahlia warned me about Gina Daily, aka Jennifer Dunston—she had a couple more aliases too as it turns out. Fortunately, I've forgotten them. I'm sure Dahlia hasn't. She won't ever let me forget what a fool I made of myself." I suddenly felt a surge of protectiveness toward him.

"Let's hope our luck has changed, Marshal." I put my arms around his neck. The gold flecks danced like flames in his dark brown eyes, and we were lost again in another of those breathless moments. Then it was my turn to laugh. "This isn't going to be easy, is it?"

"No, it won't be. I don't mind a little hard work to make the most of our change of luck, do you?"

"No."

"How about this? It's still light outside. Before we go to dinner, why don't you show me where you had so many good times with your aunt and Judy? I want to see the vineyards the way you do."

"I'd love to! I can't wait to see the little theater area. Come, Marlowe, let's go for a walk," I hollered as I slipped on my shoes, wishing once again that I'd worn a more practical pair. Spiky heels weren't exactly outdoor wear, but they do wonderful things for your legs. I could tell from Austin's appreciative stare that he noticed.

"If I topple off of these while we're roaming around in the vineyards, you'll catch me, won't you?"

"You can count on it, Calla Lily." He reached out, took my hand, and then tucked it in around his arm as we left the house.

We walked arm-in-arm across the driveway. When we crossed a stretch of lawn, we came to a gravel access road that runs along the uppermost edge of the vineyards.

"This way," I said as I walked up a small grade toward the hilly picnic spot Aunt Lettie and I had often used. The sun was riding low in the sky when we got there. I took Austin's hand and pulled him along with me until we stood between the orderly rows of grapevines. The view that stretched out below was magnificent. Marlowe was beside himself with glee as he raced around us.

"When we came here, we'd bring a picnic basket and throw a blanket on the ground over there," I said. That's when I noticed a split in the road.

"I wish I'd known you then."

"I was an anxious, skittish child—almost feral until Aunt Lettie tamed me! You might not have found much to like until she settled me down."

"I doubt that's true. Your aunt saw something in you from the beginning, didn't she?"

"I suppose so. How about you? Were you always a wild child?"

"Unfortunately, yes. My grandparents had a hard time keeping me out of trouble. If I'd stayed with them instead of going back and forth to my parents, I might have decided to stay on the right side of the law sooner. My dad was a big drinker, and I got the idea in my head that I could show him up by out-drinking him. That didn't go over well as you can imagine. Eventually, my grandparents' steady hands paid off—or maybe it was my grandpa's hand on my troublesome behind."

"I'm glad something worked for us, and we figured out

a way to channel our wild streaks. For me, acting the part of a relentless troublemaker, and for you tracking them down. What you do is important. It's too bad what you do is so dangerous."

"It can be. Most of the time, it's a more routine process of hunt, stalk, and capture than what went on at the resort. Sometimes, fugitives are so fed up with running and hiding that they don't put up a fight at all." I was about to speak when I thought I heard rustling in the vines. I went on alert and was on the verge of shushing Austin when Marlowe popped out of the vines carrying a stick. I sighed with relief. Austin bent down, wrestled the stick free, and gave it a toss. Marlowe took off after it.

"This is my favorite time of the day at my favorite spot in my favorite place on earth. I love the way the setting sun covers everything in a golden glow. When I was growing up here, this is when I felt rich. To me, it was a fairyland of vines dipped in gold." Austin put an arm around me, and we stood for a minute basking in the warmth of that glow. Marlowe bounded back again, having retrieved the stick. Austin tossed it again, and Marlowe darted after it. I suggested we follow him.

"Let's go take a peek at the theater, and then we'll have dinner, I promise." I grabbed Austin's hand and pulled him back to the road running along the vineyards which would take us to the theater. As tired as I was, and as bad as my feet hurt, I probably should have waited until tomorrow, but I had to see it. It would be dark soon, so I picked up the pace.

"What's for dessert?" Austin asked with a wicked grin on his face.

"Don't get any ideas. After we drop off Marlowe at my room and feed him, we're going to dinner at the resort. Then, I'm going to kiss you goodnight, and send you on your way. If I can do it, I'll stand in the shower and rinse the grime away before I collapse. I'm not used to all the cops-and-robbers business—it's really creepy."

As if on cue, the shadows grew as the sun sank below the horizon. I gave Austin's hand a yank, pulling him more hastily toward the crest of the rise in the road ahead. The shadows somehow made me feel more exposed. Perhaps, because the men who'd fired at me had hidden in them.

"When you said you had an update from Rikki about the men in custody, what did you mean?"

"I was going to give you a little time to recover from the latest discussion with Dahlia. Rikki agreed to call Dahlia and fill her in. Both men claim they don't know the identity of the person who hired them. They don't have a motive either. Apparently, that doesn't seem to matter in the murder for hire business. In any case, only one of the men, Aldon Kutchner—the fugitive I was following—was hired to kill you. He picked up his partner, who's a local, because the guy knew his way around the woods and the resort."

"Is that how they got onto the property without alerting security?" I asked, stopping for a second to take in this newest clue about what had occurred at the resort.

"Yes. The gun-happy amateur with Kutchner fired most of the rounds once I mucked with their plan to take you out with a single shot. It created a distraction that Kutchner tried to use to make good on the contract to kill you."

"The shot that came from the back deck, right?"

"Yes. Here's the most valuable piece of new information. The first of two payments promised to Kutchner was wired to him. The wire was traced to an offshore shell company."

"Great!" I said as I began walking again. "Now you're telling me there's a conspiracy behind the attempt on my life. One you'll never figure out since I'm sure any names associated with that company are fake—or it's another company that owns that one, right?"

"Something like that. Did you and your Aunt Lettie have a scheme or two up your sleeves at some point?"

"Ha ha! Not me or Aunt Lettie, but in *Not Another Day*, Andra Weis never met a scheme she didn't like. I know as much about shell companies as I do about any other dirty trick written into the script for my character over the years. I always did my homework. Understanding the world of offshore business ventures was a tough assignment. What I took away from my efforts was that shell companies work to cover up people involved in all kinds of fraudulent and illicit activities."

"They do! Sometimes, though, they leave open a back door. We have a lead from a domain site lookup service. We may have a real name for the person who registered the domain. If not, we have the IP address to trace. I'm going into the office tomorrow to help track down the culprit, and get a location in the real world, not cyberspace."

"That would be incredible if you can do it. It's probably some poor hapless webmaster."

"I hope so. A hapless webmaster won't want to take

the fall for attempted murder. Maybe it'll be a dead end, but I've got a good feeling about it. Another change of luck, Lily."

As we approached the high point in the road, I heard Marlowe barking. Then he grew quiet. When we could see what awaited us as the road sloped down again, I gasped. The man standing in the middle of the road held Marlowe in one hand and a rifle in the other.

12

Trouble in the Vines

"JESSE?" I ASKED. "What are you doing here?"

"One of the field hands, who just left, told me some-one was wandering around up here. I decided to check it out." Marlowe squirmed.

"Well, now you know who it is," Austin added. "There's no reason to worry. Lily was just showing me around before we go to dinner." Jesse's eyes narrowed as he stared at us. This time when Marlowe squirmed, he put him down on the ground.

"I'm not blind." Jesse's tone was gruff. He lowered the rifle he carried to his side.

"What are you doing out here with a rifle?" I asked. "Are you allowed to own one?" My second question got Jesse's attention.

"I take it you heard about my trouble with the law?"

"A little," I said. "A business venture that went wrong, as I understand it."

"Yes. Unfortunately, I couldn't get a judge to see it that way. In answer to your question about the rifle, I was convicted of felony possession with intent to sell. Your

Aunt Lettie hired a good lawyer for me, and the conviction got overturned. I still ended up with a misdemeanor charge, but I was released for time served, which was some kind miracle."

"A miracle named Lettie," Austin muttered. Jesse glowered at Austin and then nodded in agreement.

"Her offer of a job was another miracle. I know I don't need to tell you, Lily, that your aunt was a good woman." Jesse had switched his gaze from me to Austin when the marshal pushed Jesse to respond to my other question.

"Why are you out here toting a weapon?"

"There's been trouble in the vines," Jesse responded. "A picker told me he saw a stranger wearing a cowboy hat poking around in the vineyards. I wasn't sure who I'd meet roaming around out here at dusk, and I didn't want the sucker to run for it. I thought a rifle might persuade an unauthorized visitor to stick around and answer a few questions. Like I said, there's been some trouble lately."

"What kind of trouble?" I asked.

"Vandalism or theft—I'm not sure which. The first time I spotted a problem, I figured a picker that didn't know what he was doing had slashed the vines while picking the grapes. They weren't just cut wrong but slashed badly in places. I double-checked my records, and none of the field hands had been in the rows that day. The next day, I found new cuts in a different location, and someone had uprooted a few of the vines. The trespasser had taken a few samples of the rootstock."

"Did you report it to the police?" Austin inquired.

"Yes, but I'm not exactly buddies with members of the Calistoga Police Department."

"If you're talking about Barb Benchley, she's not a fan of mine either," I added.

"Her, yeah, but her pals don't like me any more than she does."

"What did Aunt Lettie say?"

"I was going to tell Lettie, but I didn't want her to think I couldn't handle it, so I called it in myself. They sent an officer out here who looked around, but there wasn't much to find, except a few footprints."

"Do you have any idea how someone got into the vineyards?" Austin asked.

"I checked the fences down by the road and back there along the property line." Jesse pointed behind him. "I didn't find anything. After the second incident, I checked again and found a piece of cloth stuck on the barbed wire. When I inspected the fence more closely, I could tell someone had cut the fence and then wired it back together. They didn't want to do it, but I got the cops out here again and had them pick up what looked to me like part of a flannel work shirt. They took a photo of the place where the fence was cut. What more could they do?"

"Austin has suggested we put up surveillance cameras down by the entrance gate; maybe they can be placed elsewhere in the vineyards, too. Or motion sensor lights. I don't know. Let's see what Austin suggests. Did Aunt Lettie know about this?"

"Yeah. I hated to do it since she was already worried about the fake wine she found."

"She told you about the suspected wine fraud?" Austin asked.

"Yes. She wanted me to know she was hiring someone to find the person behind it and he'd need me to explain how the vineyards operate in relation to the winery. When I told her about the vandalism, she wanted me to make sure I showed the investigator where that had occurred in case the incidents were somehow related to the fraud. She died right after that. I hope it wasn't the last straw and I gave the poor woman a heart attack."

"I promise you, Jesse, that had nothing to do with Aunt Lettie's death. I'm glad she trusted you enough to share her concerns about the bogus wine and didn't have to carry that burden alone." Just then, lights came on in the theater area behind Jesse. I sucked in my breath as the space became alive.

"It's my fairyland!" I exclaimed. I took off at a trot. When my feet screamed in pain, I kicked off my shoes and ran barefoot, as I'd done as a child. My feet weren't as calloused as they were then, and the gravel poked at them. I shifted a little to run along the grassy edge of the road, instead. Marlowe ran ahead of me.

"Lily! Wait!" Austin had yelled, as he came after me. I heard him grunt, as one of my flying shoes must have hit him.

"Sorry!" I said without stopping. When I passed through the row of trees that were lit up with all those sparkling lights, I stopped. I could see the theater now, encircled by trees lit up as if it were Christmas. Marlowe sensing my excitement, yipped, ran around me in a circle, and then dashed away. He ran back, and went through his excited routine again, this time running around all three of us.

"Now, that's the real deal." Austin laughed as Marlowe bounded around us a third time. "Marlow tested. Marlowe approved."

What I could see of the theater was amazing. The stage was set down below, surrounded by seats set up in rows as orderly as the vines. I was too stunned to trust my ability to count, but there had to be hundreds of seats!

"Normally, the lights don't come on at dusk since the theater's not in use yet. I wasn't sure what I'd find up here, so I thought a little extra light couldn't hurt depending on what I discovered. Even with the trees lit, you can't see them very well, but there are dressing rooms and prop rooms with a big barnlike workshop to build sets—classrooms, too. She went all out for you," Jesse said.

"This is my miracle, Jesse." I spun around in joy. Then the tears began for about the tenth time today. "If only I'd come home sooner. I could have shared this with Aunt Lettie!" I wailed. Without thinking, I threw myself into Austin's arms and sobbed.

"You know what they say," Jesse muttered in a low voice. "Timing is everything, isn't it?" I realized that I'd probably just put an end to Jesse's notion that we were going to rekindle our relationship—if Judy had it right. My timing might have been off again by doing that in such a thoughtless way. There was a kind of presumption in Jesse's plan that was about more than just bad timing. Like most women, though, I felt guilty. I still had to work with him.

"The theater is going to be a big boost for the vineyards, Jesse. You, Austin, and I need to get to work on rethinking security soon. We need to protect ourselves and the vines from the guests the theatrical events will bring in."

"The B&B and bake shop, too, if you decide to follow up on Lettie's plans for them." There was a hint of enthusiasm in his words. I hoped that was at the prospect of working together as business partners even if I'd dampened his expectations about romance.

It's always amazing to me how much guesswork goes on between people. When the trouble died down—here in the vines and in the rest of my trouble-prone life—I'd have another talk with Jesse. For now, my clumsy trampling of his feelings would have to do.

"If you can stand to leave this amazing place, we should go have dinner. It's been a long, hard day." Austin put an arm around my shoulders.

"It had to be. I already got a visit from a member of Calistoga's finest. They wanted me to prove where I was around lunchtime when Lettie's lawyer was killed. Fortunately, I had a couple dozen field hands to give me an alibi; otherwise, I might have been hauled in and given the third degree. Once a felon, always a felon, even when the conviction gets overturned."

"You're not the only one under suspicion. I had a Deputy U.S. Marshal and Judy vouching for my whereabouts, and Deputy Ahern still gave me the evil eye when I told her the murder weapon she found sounded just like the Bahco sharpening tool Aunt Lettie owned."

"No kidding? Was it hers? I hope so because I've got one, too. There are probably a couple more floating around here, but it'll be mine they're interested in if hers is still in the shed. You watch."

"I don't know yet. Judy took Dahlia to see if Lettie's was still in her tool shed. If it's not in there, I'll make sure Dahlia knows about the reports you filed with the Calistoga Police Department. The vandals in the vineyards need to get on the list of people who could have had access to the shed and stolen it. All we need is a host of new suspects—especially since they remain anonymous." I shook my head.

"You're right that it's time to go. I'll come back in the morning, and see what the theater looks like in the daylight." Both men flinched. "What?"

"You need to be careful, that's all," Austin replied. Jesse grunted in agreement.

"I know, I know. What a nightmare—I even have to be concerned that I'm in danger at home in broad daylight!"

"Austin's right that our security isn't what it ought to be. We're bringing in extra field hands right now," Jesse said. "At least call me or Judy or someone else to go with you rather than roam around out here alone."

"You've got the movers coming, too, remember. That means more strangers on the property. That'll make it harder for Jesse to spot a ringer in the crowd," Austin added. "I hope you vetted them."

"All right, all right. Don't gang up on me. I'm not sure what 'vetting' means when it comes to movers. I didn't just go out and hail a couple of guys off the street to help if that's what you're implying. The moving company's well-established, so I hope my possessions aren't being deliv-ered by a gang of thugs hired to kill me." I stomped my bare foot hard—not a good thing to do since we were walking on the gravel road again. "Ouch!"

"You'd better put these on." Austin handed me my shoes. I hung onto his arm and slipped them on. "Keep them handy tomorrow. If you need to defend yourself, those pointy heels could do some damage." Austin smiled as if he was kidding, but he had a point.

"I've got plenty to do tomorrow, including a few un-happy phone calls to make. I'll call Judy. Maybe she can come over and babysit me."

"Jesse will be around if you need help. I've got to go into the office in San Jose to work on a few things. We're getting closer, but I want to see where we are in the effort to find the person who paid the guys to kill you. I'll be back by dinnertime, if not before."

"Why don't we all have dinner together, and come up with a plan to revamp security? Will that work for you, Jesse?" I asked.

"Sure. The sooner, the better."

"I'm trying to get a security consultant to meet with us. He's supposed to get back to me tomorrow morning," Austin offered.

"Thanks," Jesse said, holding out his hand to shake Austin's. I sighed, hopeful that with these two on the same side, we might get through this transition.

Would it be asking too much to do that without more bloodshed? I wondered as we walked back to the driveway in the deepening shadows. The security expert couldn't get here soon enough for me. Every flutter of leaves and shift of light had me moving a little more quickly even with Austin at my side.

Our dinner was quiet. The food was delicious, and the conversation was pleasant. Austin and I agreed to spend the time learning more about each other, taking a timeout from obsessing about the odyssey of murder and mayhem we'd endured together quite by accident.

Of course, that didn't mean Austin kept his hypervigilance at bay. His eyes roamed the lovely dining room in the hotel restaurant as we were seated. He sought out the entrance to the kitchen, then found the exit signs, and scanned every spot in the room big enough to hide a killer. To be more specific, hide a killer who'd given up all pretense of stealth, and was willing to launch a brazen attack in a public place. That was my take on his behavior since he didn't say anything as our server chatted about house specialties and today's featured dishes.

The conversation we'd had as we drove to the resort focused mainly on the increased pace of events, and the bold recklessness of Franklin Everett's murderer. I dreaded not only what that might mean for me, but for Austin. His life was in danger now because of me.

Guilt took hold of me again, but not for long. Despite the dire circumstances in which we found ourselves, I relished the fact this insanely attractive, fearless, and provocative man sat across from me. That he sat here with his fingers entwined with mine was as impossible to believe as any of the other events associated with my homecoming.

When it came time to say goodnight, exhaustion won out over the temptation to drown my sorrows in Austin. Our day would start early, so after another of those tantalizing clinches filled with promise, Austin checked my suite and left. Beneath the hard-boiled, "here's lookin' at you, kid" demeanor he adopted as he tipped his hat, Austin was worried. Was it a specific worry that dogged him or the accumulated burden of the past twenty-four hours? Or was it a cop's gut feeling about what we'd face tomorrow?

13

A Harmless Little Friend

WHEN AUSTIN PICKED me up at the resort early the next morning, I almost danced at the sound of his voice. Marlowe bolted to the door ahead of me, yipping in excitement. I opened the door and found Austin standing there with a bouquet of calla lilies. My heart melted as he stepped into the room. I took the flowers he held out and threw my arms around his neck, covering his face in kisses before our lips met.

"You're so sweet! They're amazing. I'm going to put them on the table in the dining room where you'll have dinner with me tonight." I was a little sad that we'd invited Jesse, too, but at least Austin and I would be together.

"I can hardly wait! You'll be the most beautiful calla lily in the room." His breath was warm as he spoke those words into my ear. "You smell like a flower, too. Let's get you home before I forget I have a job to do today. I'm sure the hotel will be happy for me to move my truck that's parked in the loading zone out front." I tore myself away. Clutching those flowers, I felt silly like a high school girl reveling in the corsage her prom date had given her. It had been a long time since a man had brought me flowers. Tony wasn't big on the idea, although he did give me jewelry—usually when he'd done something wrong.

"I'm all packed and ready to go. I woke up early, and decided to get organized."

"I wish I didn't have to leave you alone today," Austin said as he grabbed the bags near the door. I picked up a satchel that doubled as a purse and an overnight bag. I slipped the strap onto my shoulder so I could carry Marlowe and those lovely flowers.

"Hey, you're a busy lawman hunting down desperados. My case can't be the only one you're working on. Given how fast the bodies are piling up, you've gotten yourself roped into a bigger mess than you ever dreamed possible when you tracked that hired gunman here." I dashed after him as he stepped into the elevator.

"Nothing's more important than getting to the bottom of the mess you're in. I'll admit that at this point, we're talking about three or four cases rather than one. Rikki and I may be able to help with the fraud issue. We tracked down a guy not long ago who was engaged in counterfeiting and wine theft in this area. He's behind bars. It could be that the crew that's vandalizing the Calla Lily Vineyards, and putting out trashy wine under what looks like your label, has ties to the setup he ran before he left wine country for the Coachella Valley."

The elevator pinged, and we stepped out and headed down the hall and through the lobby. I waved as we passed the front desk without stopping since I'd checked out online using their TV set. There weren't any charges—

not even for my dinner last night with Austin. I appreciated the gesture, but it was small compensation for the close call I'd had the night before last. As soon as we reached his truck, Austin picked up where he'd left off.

"The guy I'm talking about didn't think twice about vandalism either, so maybe the incidents in the vineyards are connected to the fraud. Before he fled the area, the maniac set fire to the outbuilding where the phony wine was stored." Austin opened the back door of his truck and stowed my bags. "That fire destroyed acres of the nearby vineyards and killed a man, so the fugitive we picked up in Mexico is now serving time for arson and murder, as well his other crimes."

Austin opened the door for me and held onto Marlowe. I slid my bag inside, climbed into the passenger seat, and held out my arms for my happy pooch, who was giving Austin a kiss or two.

"Your fugitive who's now in prison is a good example of a one-man crime spree, isn't he?" I asked.

"Yes, although he also had a gang of lowlifes working for him. Some of them are already back on the street. That's who we'll be rounding up to chat with about the counterfeit wine business." Austin shut my door, ran around to the driver's side, and hopped into his seat. Once he'd buckled up and checked the area around us, we took off.

"I gave this crime spree some thought when I woke up at dawn and couldn't go back to sleep. I'd forgotten how much racket the birds make here as the sun rises. Where are all the traffic noises that cover up their squawking?" I asked.

"Spoken like a woman who's spent too much time in the big city." Austin gave me a teasing wink and a big grin.

"My country girl roots are still intact. I hope. No more six-inch heels."

"Hey, there's no need to be too hasty and give up all your big city ways. They looked great on you with that dress." Austin beamed a roguish smile.

"How about this? No more stiletto heels in the vineyards or on gravel roads. I trashed the pair I wore yesterday after only one day of treating them like hiking boots. I'll keep the others for indoor use, or for a special occasion." That drew an enthusiastic nod from Austin. I had more to say. "If you think they looked great with the dress I wore yesterday, wait until you see six-inch heels with this slinky little cocktail dress a designer gave me to wear to an Academy Awards party last year. When I say little, I mean short. So short, you'd think I was a six-foot supermodel." Austin had grown quiet. I saw him gulp. I'm pretty sure I'd rendered him speechless. When he glanced at me, I raised an eyebrow and gave him my best version of a roguish smile.

"Mercy, woman. We're in the middle of a murder investigation. You need me to keep my wits about me, so no more stories about short dresses and tall heels. I'm only human, Lily."

"If you insist, Marshal. You started it."

"So, I did." He laughed.

"As I was saying, when I went over all the events, I couldn't help feeling this is a well-orchestrated attack on the Calla Lily Vineyards and Winery. It's not just the murder of Aunt Lettie and her lawyer. The vandalism and fraud could be a way to undermine production and damage the brand. Then again, the dirty deeds have been undertaken in such an incoherent way, it's almost as if the orchestra's not playing the same song."

Austin said nothing as we drove through the rolling hills which were alive with color and motion. Even at this early hour, work was underway in some of the fields. Perhaps Austin was deep in thought pondering my words about the nature of the villainy we were up against. I saw him glance a time or two in his rearview mirror. I did the same using my side mirror. Was Eddie Callahan barreling down the road after us in his Caddy? I didn't see a thing. Austin finally broke the silence.

"Even the best-planned conspiracies fall apart when the desperation that set the game in motion reaches a point where it becomes an 'every man for himself' affair. Maybe this started out as a coordinated strike, and rapidly deteriorated into a free-for-all."

"Okay, so if this was a coordinated effort, what do they want?" I asked.

"I'm not sure yet. I've been trying to put it all together, too. If Lettie was murdered, that's where this started— with your aunt's death rather than the attempt on your life. What makes the most sense to me is that you're the reason the plan fell apart. Once you arrived, you were supposed to be out of the way immediately. The attack took place even before the reading of the Will, so it may or may not have been about someone getting their hands on your inheritance or Lettie giving you control of her shares. When you weren't killed as planned, the partnership came unglued."

"Whoever went after Franklin in such a brutal way was unglued, that's for sure."

"Yeah, but what person in their right mind hires a hitman to begin with?" As Austin asked that question, I flashed on the image of the grim-faced, white-knuckled Alexander Davidson. His demeanor was so out of line with the control exuded by the cut of his suit—tailor-made, no doubt. Every hair was in place; his manicure perfect. Had Aunt Lettie become an annoying imperfection he could no longer tolerate?

"Or gives an overdose of medication to a kindhearted, energetic woman like Aunt Lettie if that's what happened to her." Austin grew silent again. He checked his side mirror and his rearview mirror as he'd done previously.

"What is it?" I asked when he slowed down and then checked again. This time when I looked in my side mirror, I spotted a car. My heart rate picked up when it kept coming. Then the driver must have hit the brakes because it almost instantly receded into the distance.

"Someone may be tailing us," Austin replied. "She's hanging back. If I'm not mistaken, it's either sweet young thing one or sweet young thing two."

"Can't you catch her or let her catch us or let her think she's caught us?"

"Then what?" Austin asked.

"I don't know exactly. You're packing heat. Tell her to drop her weapon, come clean, or you'll help her advance to a higher level of consciousness by opening her third eye quick." Austin glanced sideways at me and shook his head.

"That has to be a line you took from a Hollywood script!"

"From Andra's wicked lips to your ears, my dear." He shook his head again and laughed.

"I'm going to let Dahlia catch her. When I slowed down coming around the curve in the road a while ago, she didn't. Before she realized she needed to back off, she got close enough for me to read her license plate numbers. I'll text Dahlia as soon as we get you into the house. You brought your transponder gizmo, didn't you? I don't want to loiter too long at the gate. What if our harmless little friend is packing heat, too?"

"My money is on you, Marshal. You could outdraw her if it came to a showdown."

"Lily, you may have been in character as Andra a little too long for your own good," Austin said. "What we lawmen try to do is avoid showdowns and shootouts, especially with a lovely, Hollywood vixen along as a sidekick. Dahlia has to interview her anyway. Let her track her down, bring her in, and ask her a few more questions about why she's following us at such an early hour."

Minutes later, when we pulled up to the gate, it opened immediately since I'd done as Austin suggested and whisked out my transponder. When we drove onto the property, Jesse was standing outside the bunkhouse, surrounded by field hands.

The gate closed behind us, and I expelled a breath of air I hadn't even been aware I'd been holding. My breathing had barely returned to normal, when a car slowed down out on the road we'd just left. The car made a right turn into the entrance across the road from us. I startled when Austin tapped his horn a couple times. Marlowe looked up at me as if wondering if he should be worried. *He ought to be worried about me since I was a basket case.*

"Is that the car you saw tailing us?" I asked.

"What car?" Austin asked as he checked his rearview mirror, and waved at Jesse. Jesse waved back as we drove on up the hill. The car was long gone.

"Never mind. I'm jumpy. A car turned into the winery entrance across the road, that's all."

Austin parked close to the front door. I opened my door, and Marlowe dove out of the truck. He was up the steps and on the porch by the time I slid out of my seat. Austin was at my side by then, scanning the area around us. I reached in and grabbed my bag and those flowers.

"Let's get you inside, and then I'll text Dahlia. Once we're sure she's got that license plate, it'll ease your mind. Before I leave, I'll haul the rest of your stuff in. Did you bring in the items from the trunk of your car yesterday?"

"Yes. I parked my car in the garage, brought everything in, and stashed it in the closet just off the foyer," I replied warily looking around me as I opened the front door to Aunt Lettie's house. Austin did a quick inspection downstairs, dashing down the hallway to the right as he typed a text to Dahlia. When he came back to the foyer, I heard a whoosh as he sent the text.

"I need to put these in water," I said, following him to the kitchen. While Austin checked the cellar, I filled a vase with water and set the flowers on the center island in the kitchen for now. The flowers seemed to bring life and hope into the room.

Would this place ever really feel like home again? I wondered as Austin ran up the steps from the cellar and closed the door. He checked the locks on the door leading out back from the kitchen.

"Be sure to keep these locked today, okay?"

"I will."

"Let's move upstairs, so I can make sure no one's been in here since last night." As he headed upstairs, he carried a couple of items from the closet.

In jeans and sensible shoes, I was in much better shape for a day that was going to involve lots of hauling. With Marlowe urging us on from the top, I hustled behind Austin with my overnight bag and a zippered hanging bag I'd taken from the closet and draped over my shoulder. I was a little out of breath when we arrived at what had once been my room.

Like the rest of the house, this room had been given a makeover, but Aunt Lettie had kept my personal items much as I'd left them. My favorite thing about the room was completely unchanged. The morning sunlight streamed in through large windows.

The windows were now positioned on either side of a newly-installed set of French doors that used to be a solid wall. The doors opened out onto a small wrought iron balcony. Austin set down the bags and gaped at the view. I dropped the load I carried onto my bed and motioned for him to follow me out onto the balcony.

From there, we could see over the vineyards to the Calla Lily Winery across the road. The Welcome Center that sat back some distance from the road had once been an old stone barn with a tall silo. Lettie's architect had transformed them into what appeared to be a small fortress guarded by a turret.

Wine production and storage buildings were on one side of the Welcome Center. Offices and rooms for large gatherings were on the other side. A huge courtyard out front and gardens in the back provided places to entertain al fresco. The grounds were surrounded by rambling stone fences with large iron gates that were closed and locked at night. The darkness we were facing suddenly rose up like storm clouds hovering above the lovely scene. Austin must have experienced something like that, too, or he sensed the shift in my mood because he reached out to take my hand.

I stared at the winery wondering if Alexander Davidson was sitting in his office right now. Did he convey the same impression he'd tried to achieve at the reading of the Will—that of a well put-together, self-possessed man? Or did he fail now, too, and give himself away as a man on the verge of dissembling?

Had that already happened and he'd murdered Franklin in a momentary loss of control? I shuddered at the possibility that the man who may have tried to have me killed, who killed Aunt Lettie and her lawyer, could be right across the road. I gripped the railing on the balcony as if that would keep me from falling into Alexander Davidson's clutches.

14

A Toxic Brew

"ONE OF THE things I'm going to do today is run down whatever background information I can find about both Connie Laughton and Carol Matheson. It occurred to me when I was lying awake last night—thinking more about you than crime or criminals, to be honest—that it's a little odd that both your aunt and her lawyer were probably killed by people they knew. There wasn't any sign of a break-in or a struggle at either location. We know sweet young thing one and sweet young thing two *weren't* at the crime scenes on the days Lettie and Franklin died. If Dahlia can interview either one of them, it might help figure out where they were."

"It is strange, isn't it, that on the days they died, they were each expected to visit and didn't show up? I kept getting them mixed up in my mind last night. From the way people have described them, they share physical characteristics, but it's more about how well they both fit your profile as harmless creatures who wouldn't hurt a living soul. You couldn't figure out which one was in the car behind us today either." I searched the cars in the lot across the way, hoping I could identify the car I'd seen turn in there.

"Was the car you saw tailing us a white, two-door compact?" I asked.

"A white compact is correct, but I couldn't tell you if it was a two-door or four-door. Why?"

"That's the car I asked you about that was there one minute and gone the next. It turned into the winery shortly after we turned in here. I don't see it in the lot now, but maybe it's behind the carriage house or those trees," I said pointing at a line of trees in front of the office building.

"I could be wrong, and the car I thought was following us was headed to the winery instead."

"When we asked Jesse if he recognized the woman he spoke to as Carol Matheson and he said he wasn't sure, we didn't ask about the car she drove. If he ever opened the gate for Carol Matheson, he ought to remember if she drove a white, two-door compact sedan, don't you think? He didn't mention it, but we could ask him the same question about the car driven by the woman who tried to get in here yesterday."

"I'll ask Jesse on my way out if he's still hanging around down there near the gate. If he says anything about a white compact sedan, I'll text Dahlia about it."

"Here's another point, though. I'd be stunned if, after her first visit or two, Lettie didn't give Carol Matheson the gate code to let herself in. If it was Carol coming to see me because Judy had called her, why stop at the gate like that? Connie Laughton's another matter. If she's the one who butchered Franklin and made a couple of lame efforts to frame me for it, she may have wanted to get in here, and pick up another memento of my existence to plant in a strategic spot."

"I'm not convinced your sunglasses were part of a set-up intended to frame you. Who could have known ahead of time that you'd leave them there? That makes me wonder if the weapon used was aimed at setting up someone else. Jesse told us last night that he has one like it. With his police record, he's an easier mark than you are if the killer wanted to frame someone."

"When Judy gets here, I'll ask if Lettie's sharpening tool was missing."

"If the police can link that tool to Jesse, he moves up higher on the list of suspects in Lettie's death, too, if it turns out there's enough evidence to prove she was murdered."

"Jesse sure qualifies as someone Aunt Lettie would have regarded as harmless. Maybe it's because Jesse's an old friend and the sweet young things aren't, but it's easier for me to concede that one or both of the women are murderers rather than Jesse."

"Dahlia's already convinced there's more than one killer involved, but two, plus the guys paid to go after you, is hard to believe except in the context of a conspiracy. Dahlia and I have talked in the past about how hard it is to make arrests and get convictions when a criminal conspiracy is involved." I gazed across the road at the winery.

"Puppets, all doing the bidding of a manipulative but not too tightly wrapped puppet master," I muttered. "And not more than a few hundred yards away." I frowned and nodded in the direction of the winery. I couldn't bear staring at the place any longer and stepped back into my suite. I turned to face Austin, making sure to make eye contact.

"I'm not sure I was as emphatic as I should have been with you or Dahlia about how disturbed Alexander Davidson was when he heard Aunt Lettie hadn't given up control of the board. What if he engineered the vandalism and fraud to harass my aunt into stepping back? Or maybe he could have used those problems to argue that Aunt Lettie was no longer up for the challenges involved in running the business. What if he planned to use the incidents to call into question her decisions to hire Jesse and Mitch Carlson and get the board to pressure her into relinquishing control?"

"If Davidson's goal is to run the business, why risk damaging the company he was so intent on controlling?"

"I know. Remember, I used the word weird. I was in Hollywood long enough to believe I can tell the difference between quirky and eccentric versus weird. Maybe the word I should have used was creepy or unnatural. That's saying a lot, too, since he was sitting in the room sur-rounded by members of the Callahan clan at the time." My mind was racing, and before Austin could say a word, I rushed on to another possibility.

"What if he's not intent on controlling the business because he's power-mad, but because he's been fiddling with the books? He could do that since he's got access to the financial accounts."

"Why not ask for a formal audit of the company books, just to make sure Davidson's not concealing problems he didn't want to share with Lettie?"

"That's a great idea. I've got a friend in LA who would be perfect for the job. At the very least, she'll help me better understand how the books are kept. Poor Jesse. At least they can't make him a scapegoat for financial troubles." Austin stepped forward and embraced me.

"Don't start feeling too sorry for him. He's still my archrival."

"Oh, please, I'm starstruck, Marshal." My playful tone turned more serious. "You have no rival, and I'll testify to that under oath." I was rewarded for my candidness with a knee-buckling kiss from Austin. I'd given him plenty of thought last night, too. My pulse had raced as I recalled moments like this one. Where they might lead was thrilling and unsettling. This had better be love because I was falling hard for the man whose gaze held me as firmly as his arms.

"Lily," was all he said along with that kiss. The way he spoke my name made me tremble. What if I never heard him say my name like that again?

"You'll be careful today, too, won't you?" I asked. "I'm not used to the idea of having a man in my life who gets shot at for a living."

"You've got my word on it. Besides, my job is about not getting shot at. If Dahlia's not already doing it, I'll get somebody to do a background check on Davidson. What about Mitch Carlson? Lettie went straight to him about the problems with the labels and wine."

"Yeah, he could have decided to shut her up before she took the matter to the board if he was behind the fraud. What about Davidson's cronies on the board? Or the maintenance crew or receptionists who greet people at the

winery Welcome Center? I'm no good at this, am I?" I
rubbed my face with both hands. "How do I trust anyone?"

"Right now, don't! Dahlia's setting up interviews and
running down alibis, and may have the staff to run the
background checks I'm proposing to do. If not, I'm on it!
Rikki and I are also working on the lead we got about the
money wired to one of the gunmen we have in custody.
The person behind the bloodbath in Franklin's office may
have slipped up and left a clue for the evidence specialists
to find as they sift through the items they've got." I tried
to take heart from the pep talk Austin was giving me. My
phone rang, cutting him off. I dug it out of the pocket
where I'd stashed it.

"Hello."

"Ms. Callahan, this is Dr. Devers with the Coroner's
Office." My heart thumped, crazily.

"Thanks for calling me, Dr. Devers."

"Dahlia said you're anxious to make arrangements for
your aunt. I'm sorry for your loss. I met her at local
functions many times. She was always a pleasure to be
around. That makes what I've got to tell you even harder
to do. The toxicology report came back, and the amount
of digoxin in her system was sky high."

"How is that possible? I understood from her friend,
Judy Tucker, that my aunt was on a relatively low dose." I
made eye contact with Austin, who nodded encouraging
me to go on.

"That's what I found when I reviewed her medical
records. Digoxin toxicity is a concern for patients who
take the drug, especially elders who use it over a pro-

longed period. There's no way so much digoxin could have entered her system by accident. Someone deliberately gave your aunt an overdose."

"Are you sure?" I asked.

"Yes. I re-examined your aunt's body, looking for an injection site this morning. I found one on the bottom of her foot. The drug must have been injected deep into the muscles to get into her system as it did. Under normal circumstances, that would have been very painful. The one bit of good news I have for you is that we also found trace amounts of chloral hydrate in your aunt's body. I doubt she felt a thing when the digoxin was administered."

"Chloral hydrate's a controlled substance," I said, mostly speaking to myself. It's the central ingredient of the classic film noir "Mickey Finn," a knockout drug that's hard to detect when slipped into a drink—like a cup of tea. I'd learned about it while carrying out another of Andra's soap opera misdeeds. It could be obtained illegally or by prescription as in the tragic circumstances surrounding Anna Nicole Smith's death. Chloral hydrate can be a toxic brew when used in combination with other drugs.

"Both the chloral hydrate and digoxin could have been obtained by prescription. There's the black market for drugs—especially controlled substances—that someone can get on the street. It's also possible both drugs were stolen from a hospital or clinic somewhere."

"Okay. Dahlia knows all this, right?" I was growing angrier by the minute as I gripped my phone.

"She does, and she's making inquiries to find out if anyone reported either drug stolen recently. It would have been a small theft so it might not have been noticed. It's an odd combination, though, so if both drugs went missing from the same location at the same time, someone might remember that."

My heart sank at the dim prospect Marcia Devers outlined. Another piece of the puzzle that couldn't quite be fit to a specific villain. Of course, I didn't miss the fact that one of the "harmless" young women we'd identified happens to be a nurse.

"Thank you for not allowing my aunt's death to be wrongly recorded as a death by natural causes. She's got a better chance of getting justice thanks to you."

"And a better chance that whoever did this won't ever do it again. I'll have a death certificate for you and will release your aunt's body to Sam Clementson this afternoon if Deputy Ahern got it right and that's what you'd like us to do."

"Yes, it is. Thanks again," I said as I hung up the phone and turned to Austin. I was too angry to cry the buckets of tears that were waiting to be spilled.

"There's no room for doubt, now. Aunt Lettie was murdered and by someone who knows how to administer a lethal injection of digoxin. A medical facility could also have given the killer access to the digoxin and a knockout drug found in my aunt's body." I explained what the coroner had said about the way the drug was given to Aunt Lettie along with the chloral hydrate.

"That puts Carol Matheson in the spotlight, doesn't it?"

"She goes to the top of my list. When Carol Matheson gives the authorities an alibi, it had better be a good one." Even though the news from Dr. Devers wasn't completely unexpected, I was still shaken, but my new chaos-driven life didn't give me time to grieve, be angry, or wallow in fear.

"Are those sirens?" I asked.

"Sounds like it to me." Austin ducked out onto the balcony.

"Please don't tell me the vineyards are on fire." I couldn't bring myself to get up off the foot of my bed where I'd slumped prepared to descend into a pity party or throw a tantrum about Aunt Lettie's murder. "I don't smell smoke," I mumbled. The screaming sirens grew closer—lots of them.

"Fire and rescue are turning in across the road. I don't smell or see smoke, so it must not be a fire. There's obviously a problem of some kind at the winery." That got me up onto my feet. I reached Austin's side just in time to see a Calistoga Police Department Patrol car turn into the winery entrance. A County Sheriff's Department SUV was on its heels, followed by a truck Austin recognized. "That's Dahlia's vehicle. I'm sorry, Lily. You sit tight. I'm going to call Rikki and let her know I'll be late for my meeting at the office. Then, I'll go across the road and find out what's going on."

"Fine." What else was I going to do given that the movers might show up any minute? As mundane as the idea seemed, someone had to be here to let them in. Besides, why take a chance on creating more tension with Alexander Davidson by showing up at the winery in the middle of a crisis? Austin was on his phone and moving at the same time.

Not another body, please no more bodies. I chanted

nonsensically to myself as I followed him downstairs to the front door.

"It's another body," Austin said. "Lock the door. I'll get back as soon as I can."

"I'm not going anywhere. My plan is to stay put, and try not to lose my mind." As I'd dashed down the stairs, trying to keep up with Austin, I almost tripped over Marlowe. I held my tiny pooch close as Austin brushed my lips with a kiss and ran to his truck. I shut the door and looked at the time on my cellphone. It was just a few minutes after eight.

"The killing starts early around here, Marlowe."

15

A Body with Wine

"**L**ET'S GET BUSY," I said, continuing my conversation with my dog. "I'm going to see if it's still simple to change the gate code, just in case Carol Matheson has the old one. We don't want anyone paying us an unannounced visit, do we?" Marlowe woofed as I went into Aunt Lettie's room to search for her laptop.

It's not unusual for me to talk to Marlowe—at least he responds to my questions. Before Tony moved out, there were lots of times I felt like I was talking to myself. Still, my conversation today was running on a bit—a testament to the stress of being part of unscripted foul play.

"It sure isn't the same as it is in the movies and on TV, huh?" Marlowe didn't respond. "You're ignoring me now, too!" Marlowe was busy nosing around, quite literally, as he scurried about in Aunt Lettie's room with his tiny snout poking into every nook and cranny. I hoped there wasn't anyone hiding under the bed or in the closet; but just in case, I scooted closer to a stand that held the fireplace tools. Could I hit someone over the head with a brass poker in real life as I'd done when my Andra character almost got what she had coming to her?

Aunt Lettie's room was almost unrecognizable. I'd never thought of it as a large room, but it seemed enormous today. The square footage hadn't changed, but the volume had. For years, Lettie had talked about ripping out the low plaster ceiling in her room. She'd finally done it, and in its place was a vaulted ceiling with vintage wooden beams.

Even though the room had changed, I could feel Aunt Lettie's presence. Pictures of the two of us lined the gorgeous mantle made of a rough-hewn beam that matched those in the ceiling. Chairs placed in front of the fireplace were the same comfy ones that had been there since I was twelve, although they'd been reupholstered in a brocade fabric that fit the Spanish Mediterranean feel of the room.

Her laptop was sitting on a bookshelf in an alcove near her desk. When I went to retrieve it, I ran my hand over the desktop that still bore the mark where I'd dropped a big rock on it. I'd been so excited when I found the gold-laced hunk of stone. "Fool's gold," she'd told me instantly, and had me read and write about it for a school project. I clutched her laptop, suddenly feeling lost without her.

I sat down by the fireplace in the chair she used to sit in while reading to me, or on occasion, telling me a story about her childhood in the "Old South," as she called it. The laptop came to life, and I had no trouble getting into her files using a variant on a "Calla Lily" passcode she'd used for as long as I could remember.

I found the instructions on how to change the gate

code in seconds and put in a new code using my phone. While I had her laptop open, I checked Aunt Lettie's email. I scanned the messages she'd received recently, not sure what I expected to find. I smiled when I reviewed our latest exchange.

I didn't find any messages that appeared even remotely threatening, although I didn't take the time to read each of them carefully. If she and Alexander Davidson were at odds over anything, they didn't carry on about it by email.

The only items that piqued my curiosity were emails from my mother in the past couple of weeks. I read them to see if Dottie Callahan had hit up the poor woman for money recently. There were almost a dozen emails over the past three months. There may have been more that went back even farther in time, but that's all I could stand to read. Aunt Lettie's responses were always cheerful, encouraging, and brief.

My mother's emails were filled with gossip. She bad-mouthed family members. Those on her side of the family garnered the bulk of her attention, but Eddie's brothers and an uncle caught it, too. Dottie's observations read more like a high school mean girl than a woman well into midlife. Her comments were totally narcissistic and self-serving.

How unstable is she? I wondered. A few emails devolved into nasty rants. She made numerous references to the wasteful spending and stinginess of other family members while exempting my aunt: "Unlike you, Lettie, they don't understand what's involved in raising children under trying circumstances."

I wondered what trying circumstances meant and

forced myself to read a few earlier emails. In one, Dottie referred to her own courage given "the difficult transition we face as Eddie leaves his old job and starts a new one." I read that sentence aloud.

"What do you think, Marlowe?" He'd jumped up in the chair near mine, and was dozing contentedly. When I spoke, he opened his bleary eyes, yawned, and whined at the same time. "A yawn and a whine—I couldn't agree with you more!" Then he put his head down, thumped his tail, and resumed his nap.

Dottie expressed plenty of smarmy sentiment toward Aunt Lettie replete with what I can only describe as baby talk. She never thanked Aunt Lettie outright for her generosity or explicitly mentioned a loan or a gift of money, but there were veiled references that made me certain that if I kept searching, I'd find something about the loan Aunt Lettie had forgiven in her Will. Perhaps in response to a plea from my mother amid wailing and gnashing of teeth about Eddie losing his job. I doubted she'd given Aunt Lettie a truthful version of what he'd done to lose his job. Was my mother any more honest when she said Eddie was starting a new one?

"What do you think Dahlia has dug up about Eddie Callahan's whereabouts when Franklin was killed? Maybe Eddie's unhappiness at the reading of the Will was more about desperation than greed." Marlowe didn't open his eyes, but my comments provoked a couple more tail thumps.

I strained my brain, but I couldn't come up with anything Eddie could have hoped to achieve by meeting with Franklin. Even if Eddie had suddenly discovered a Codicil or something as ridiculous, Franklin wouldn't have bought it for a second. The snippet Franklin had read yesterday: "revoking all Wills and Codicils previously made" instantly sprang to mind. Not even Eddie could be dumb enough to believe he'd get around that pronouncement. My stepfather was back on my list of suspects, though.

"Well, how do you like that!" I exclaimed loud enough that poor Marlowe sprang to his feet. When I checked Aunt Lettie's calendar, I discovered a surprise. It wasn't on her Google calendar but on the one linked to the Calla Lily Vineyards and Winery for internal use by board members.

"Just like the one at the studio," I muttered. It was used to coordinate the schedules of all the actors, writers, and other staff who were key to the production of *Not Another Day*.

Since Aunt Lettie was already signed in, I'd had no trouble getting into the company intranet. What caught my eye was that for the past month, Aunt Lettie had regularly scheduled meetings with Carol Matheson—twice a week. That included one on the day she died that Aunt Lettie hadn't canceled. I grabbed my phone and called Austin. When he didn't pick up, I decided to wait a few minutes and try again.

While I waited, I skimmed through Lettie's calendar wondering when the last board meeting was held and when she last met with Alexander Davidson. Board meetings were scheduled regularly for the fourth Wednesday of the month. The early hour of those meetings evoked dread, given the late nights I'd kept for more than a decade in LA. At least, I'd only have to stumble across the road to get to the meetings.

Besides the board meetings, Aunt Lettie had met with Mitch Carlson, but not Alexander Davidson. I checked out what was being said "in-house" about the Calla Lily Vineyards and Winery. Pages and pages were dedicated to staff directories, employee handbooks, and forms used by human resources. Production reports and minutes from previous board meetings were also accessible, given my aunt's status in the corporation. It was all dry stuff.

I had a few teeth-gritting moments when I perused the public relations materials in which photos of Alexander Davidson appeared. Especially one in which a phony smile was plastered on his face as he watched Aunt Lettie handing out awards to bright-eyed high school grads. My eyes grew cloudy with tears at the obvious happiness the moment brought to Aunt Lettie and those kids who weren't much older than I'd been when the woman changed my life.

I dabbed at my eyes with the corner of a sleeve. When my eyes cleared again, I noticed a name in the footer at the bottom of the webpage. My guts churned, and I called Austin again.

Where is he? I wondered. I was growing more anxious about what might be going on over there. The sirens had stopped, and I hadn't heard gunfire, but there had to be trouble—big trouble to keep Austin away from his phone. Just as I was about to leave a message, Austin said hello.

"Austin, I won't keep you long. I've got news—for Dahlia and maybe something for you and Rikki."

"Okay—you haven't been out roaming around playing sleuth, have you?"

"No, this is strictly armchair snooping." Austin sighed when I rattled off the stuff I'd found.

"That's really good work. I'm sure now that the coroner has ruled Lettie's death a homicide, Dahlia or Barb will want you to turn over her laptop." I felt a twinge in my heart given how close it seemed to bring me to Aunt Lettie. As I read its contents, it was almost as if I was part of her life again.

"Will I get it back?"

"Yes. Once the investigation into Lettie's death is over, you'll get it back. Although, they'll also want to make sure there's nothing of value on it related to Franklin Everett's death."

"Great, then you and Rikki can get to work tracking down who contracted with the web host listed here that just happens to be the same one tied to the account that wired money to a hitman. Why not march into Alexander Davidson's office, and ask him point blank if he did it?"

"I wish I could. We'll have to figure out someone else to ask about it, Lily." By the tone in Austin's voice, I knew the answer to my question already, but I asked it anyway.

"He's dead, isn't he?"

"Yes."

"How?" I asked.

"Drowned in wine."

"That can't be—there are precautions taken everywhere in the winery—not just in the fermentation room. I'm not sure what he would have been doing in there anyway. There's no place in the entire winery that a barrel or a tank's left open."

"Alexander Davidson was found in a storage area at

the back with old oak barrels that aren't used anymore. I guess they're barrels that are sold to people who repurpose them or use the wood. He was found upside down in a huge barrel that had about six inches of wine in the bottom. Obviously, he didn't just fall in."

"Was his head bashed in like Franklin's?"

"No. The coroner suspects he was sedated and then stuffed into the barrel to drown. The evidence specialists found a bottle of what's probably more fake wine. Most of it had spilled onto the floor, but they hope there's still enough in it to test for the presence of a sedative. Davidson hasn't been dead long, so there might also be enough in his bloodstream to detect it."

"The few remaining circuits in my brain just fizzled out. I don't get it. I was sure Davidson was the mastermind of a plot to get rid of me, Aunt Lettie, and her lawyer."

"That could be true. He wouldn't be the first mastermind to end up dead when his minions turned on him."

"Who could it be? Nurse Matheson, the sweet young thing who knows about sedatives and other drugs, couldn't have stuffed him in the barrel like that—not without help. I don't see how she's connected to the wine fraud, either, do you?"

"No. The car you saw turning in here earlier is gone, but it does fit the description of the car bearing the license plate numbers I gave Dahlia. That car was a rental."

"Don't keep me in suspense. To whom was it rented, Marshal?"

"Not the nurse, but the other sweet young thing— Connie Laughton. The car's not here now. There's no sign of her, either, although someone vaguely remembers seeing a person who fits her description walking across the parking lot toward the production area. I suppose she could be tied into the fraud."

"Still, she's no more capable of hefting Davidson into a wine barrel head first than Carol Matheson. Has Dahlia picked her up for questioning?"

"Not yet. She hasn't been able to reach her or Carol Matheson. Connie Laughton came into town about a week ago. She's been staying at a B&B not far from here, but she checked out yesterday."

"So, if she was a visitor from out of town, does that mean she's on her way home now?"

"I checked a few minutes ago, and the car hasn't been returned to the rental agency. The driver's license she used to rent the car was issued by the state of Virginia. When she reserved her suite at the B&B, she gave them a home address in Richmond."

"How about Carol Matheson? She hadn't been working as Aunt Lettie's nurse for very long. Has Dahlia found out more about her?"

"A little. She's been in the area for a few months and lives in an apartment near the medical center where she works in Calistoga. Carol Matheson is still using her Maryland driver's license."

"If Dahlia hasn't spoken to either Carol or Connie, does that mean she hasn't been able to establish an alibi for either one of them at the time Aunt Lettie or Franklin were killed?"

"As it turns out, the owner of the B&B, Dianne Hardy, claims Connie Laughton complained about feeling ill after lunch that day. She remembers it very clearly because she was concerned about getting hit with an accusation that she was sickened by tainted food. Her worry about getting sued was tied to the fact she knew Connie Laughton was in town meeting with a lawyer. She said it had to do with property in the area, but Beth Varner thought she was meeting with Franklin about a family matter. According to Dianne Hardy, Connie Laughton told her the fresh air made her feel better, and she spent most of the afternoon reading on the patio."

"What she was doing at Franklin's law office ought to be easy enough to figure out once Beth gets the mess cleaned up and can go through his files. I hope it wasn't one of the files on his desk in the pool of blood or isn't missing!"

"Dahlia says Beth's not in great shape. Franklin's associates have hired someone to help her. These things take time which seems to be our biggest enemy right now."

"That and whoever seems intent on demonstrating the ability to commit homicide by every known method." I paused to take a deep breath. "Connie Laughton's alibi sounds legit, doesn't it?"

"Yeah, it does. Dahlia said the Hardy woman had no doubt she was sick because Connie Laughton didn't look right."

"Okay, so what about Carol Matheson?"

"Her immediate supervisor claimed she was at work that day—subbing for another nurse at an elder day care center."

"Would she have canceled an appointment with Aunt Lettie to do that?"

"That's a good question for Dahlia to ask when she brings her in for an interview. Lettie could have canceled the meeting—maybe in person the last time she and Carol Matheson met since there's no evidence a call or message was exchanged between them that day."

"That's possible, I guess. Whoever hired Carol must have checked her credentials to make sure she really is a nurse. If she'd had any kind of trouble with the law—like stealing drugs from a previous workplace—it should have turned up during the hiring process."

"You'd think so."

"What do you make of the fact that Carol was still on Aunt Lettie's calendar at the winery?" I asked.

"Your aunt was a busy woman, with plenty on her mind. She must have forgotten to remove it from the work calendar. I do that sometimes—make a change one place and forget to fix it somewhere else."

"True, but I was always more concerned about correcting appointments on my calendar at the studio since it's such a headache to coordinate twenty or thirty schedules. Something was weird about the fact that the phone was gone, and then magically reappeared the next day. What if the killer took it to remove the appointment and any texts or messages sent between her and Lettie that day and then put it back?"

"You still have Carol Matheson pegged as the guilty party, despite her alibi, don't you?"

"I'm having a tough time letting it go considering how Aunt Lettie died. It doesn't make sense, though, does it?" I sighed. "What are you going to do next?"

"It's still in my plans today to dig into Carol Matheson

and Connie Laughton's backgrounds a little more. I wish someone had a license plate number for the car you saw turn in here this morning. That way we'd be more certain Connie Laughton was roaming around here close to the time Alexander Davidson was killed. She still needs to explain what she was doing on the road in this area, and where she was when Davidson was murdered."

"Does anybody know what Alexander Davidson was doing in that storage area?"

"No. He told his secretary that he was stepping out for a few minutes, and would be right back. She thought he might have received a call on his cellphone since he was holding it as he left. The evidence specialists are still at the crime scene. So far, there's no sign of his phone."

"Dahlia can get the call records from his carrier, right?"

"Yes. She's already working on it. I'll pass along the information you came up with about Lettie's calendar, and I'll tell Dahlia your stepdad's a bigger loser than you already figured."

"I didn't say that, but it's true, isn't it? If he hasn't left town yet, Dahlia still has time to ask him all about the job change and how 'trying' his 'difficult transition' has been. I wouldn't be astonished to learn that he and Dottie are lying, and he doesn't have a new job at all. He wasn't close to Aunt Lettie, so why ask for time off soon after taking a new position to come out here?"

"Were the Callahans planning to attend the funeral?" Austin asked.

"No. Franklin told me the uncertainty about a burial date made it impossible for them to plan—something like that. It's my understanding they were going to leave soon, but I don't know how soon."

"Dahlia's on it, I'm sure. I'll ask her what she's found out when I tell her what financial straits the Callahans were in—maybe even after your aunt gave them all that money."

"I wonder if Alexander Davidson's secretary knows who contracted with the web host they're using, and who designed their site. She must know who handles techie matters for the company. The movers still haven't shown up so I could call her if you need to get going."

"Don't do that. I'm as curious as you are, and already planned to ask before I leave. So far, no one involved in this mess wants me dead. You may still be on the hit list, Lily." I couldn't argue with that since the killing wasn't over yet. "How are you holding up, by the way?"

"I'm numb, or maybe I disliked Alexander Davidson so much that it's hard to get worked up about his death."

"You've spent the past couple of days wondering if he hired two gunmen to kill you. I wouldn't blame you if you felt a little relieved that he's dead. Even if it turns out he didn't hire hitmen, he wasn't going to make your life easy."

"When you put it like that, I should be happy I'm not a suspect in his murder. I do have a solid alibi though since I was making out with Deputy U.S. Marshal Jennings around the time someone drowned him in wine. I've heard of a wine with body, but a body with wine is new."

"Even without Davidson hassling you, you've got a hell of a mess on your hands once you take your place on the Board of Directors. Besides the wine fraud, you've got security problems here as well as in the vineyards. No one has any idea how someone got into the storage area, killed Davidson, and got out again without being seen."

"Please, stop! I've been talking to Marlowe like he's a human. When I came into Aunt Lettie's room, I was so spooked that I tried to remember how I wielded a fireplace poker to fend off a jilted wife with a loaded gun in *Not Another Day*. Now, I'm making stupid jokes about bodies and wine—isn't it obvious I'm whacked?"

"Your sense of humor is still intact," Austin said, laughing at my tirade.

"I didn't have any problem establishing my alibi a while ago, either, did I?"

"No, you did not. I'll testify to that under oath, too, if necessary."

"Am I going to get put to the test again before dinnertime?" I asked, as I stood up, stretched, and looked around the room. Aunt Lettie's bookshelves were loaded with books.

"I've got an appointment with Rikki that I need to keep—especially if I can find someone here to give us information about the web host and maybe even point us to a physical location for the webmaster. I'm going to be lucky to get there on time if I also touch base with Dahlia. I'll get back to you before dinnertime if I can." He sighed. "The movers are going to pull up out front any minute now. You'll get more done without me hanging onto you."

"Sad, but true. If they don't get here soon, they won't even have the truck unloaded by the time you get back. Go find the bad guys while I try to figure out where to put all the stuff that shouldn't even be in the moving van anyway."

"Where's Judy? I thought she was going to help you figure out how to do that?"

"She has her own chores to do. If she's not here when the van pulls up, I'll call her. Don't worry; I'm sure she'll be here any minute now." Just then, I spotted a stack of photo albums on the bottom shelf. Next to them was Aunt Lettie's Bible.

"Will do. I'll call you if I get the bad guys, or have something to tell you that can't wait."

"It's a deal," I said, feeling a bit distracted as I bent down and wiggled the Bible free from where it was wedged in between other books. "And, Austin..."

"Yes?"

"Thank you. I don't know what I'd do without you."

"That goes for me too, Calla Lily." As I hung up the phone, the Bible shifted in my hand, the cover fell open, and a sheet of paper floated to the floor.

"What on earth?" I asked as I picked it up and tried to fathom what I'd just found.

16

In their DNA

WHY WOULD AUNT Lettie have a page of DNA results from what appeared to be a paternity test tucked away in her Bible? I opened the cover to see if there were other pages that might explain what it meant. There weren't any names listed anywhere—just a table that included a column for mother, child 1 and child 2, and a father with numbers listed in each column.

Even though I didn't find more pages of a DNA report with names, several names Aunt Lettie had written under "FAMILY RECORD" jumped out at me. Each name entered in the family registry was written first in Lettie's flowing script. Next to it, she'd entered the name again in print. Her own name was there, along with those of her grandparents, parents, and siblings. Their birthdates were listed, as well as the dates when some of them had died.

The Laughton name blared at me from the pages. Ann's mother, Lettie's sister, was originally listed as Emma Caroline Morgan. Aunt Lettie had added the last name Laughton to Emma's name years ago. She'd added Emma's husband's name, too—William Elliot Laughton—and then carefully drawn a straight red line through his name several years later. She'd done the same to Emma's married name.

Emma and William had a daughter—Ann Letitia Laughton. She was born in 1952, while Aunt Lettie was living with Emma. The date Aunt Lettie's niece died was penned in small print next to her name. She was only fifty-two years old. It all fit perfectly with the story Judy had told me.

Although Ann Letitia Laughton never changed her name, apparently, she married for a brief period and had a daughter, Caroline Ann Medford. She must be the "grandniece" for whom Aunt Lettie had set up a trust fund years ago. Aunt Lettie had drawn a line through Harry Medford's name. My skin prickled when I saw the Laughton name pop up again. Caroline Ann Medford became Caroline Ann Laughton after her divorce.

What had happened to Aunt Lettie's grandniece, Caroline Ann Laughton? There was no indication that she'd died. Born in 1975, she'd only be forty-three now. The last name couldn't be a coincidence—Connie Laughton had to be her daughter. An image of the tea set boxed up and ready to be mailed floated into my mind, along with Judy's question. *"Have you called Emma, yet?"*

I dreaded calling Aunt Lettie's sister, but it had to be done. She needed to know what had happened to Aunt Lettie—all of it. I needed to verify my hunch that Connie Laughton was a relative. When I dialed the number for Emma, an officious sounding woman answered.

"Willoughby Arms, how may I help you?"

"I hope I'm calling the correct number. I'm trying to

reach my aunt, Emma Morgan."

"You've called the right place. Let me see if she's in her room or at lunch. I'm going to put you on hold."

The address for Emma Morgan was in an apartment complex in Maryland. Lunch hour was just coming to an end on the East Coast. My stomach fluttered with dread and apprehension as I waited. Aunt Lettie's older sister is in her mid-eighties. What if the bad news I had to share with her was more than she could handle? Still, it seemed worse to let her learn about her sister's death and the circumstances surrounding it some other way. Via motormouth Dottie Callahan, for example.

"Emma speaking. Who's this?" She asked in a lively tone that gave me the sense that she was more curious than wary. Her voice was reminiscent of Aunt Lettie's but bore even more of a southern drawl.

"Aunt Emma, it's Lily—Lily Callahan." There was silence on the other end. When Emma responded her voice was somber.

"Is Lettie sick or dead?"

"Dead," I replied almost in a whisper, fighting hard not to cry.

"How?"

"Her heart gave out."

"What was she doing—trying to ride a bucking bronco or redo the roof all by herself?"

"No. I hate to bring you such awful news, but Aunt Lettie's heart stopped because someone intentionally gave her an overdose of medication."

"Murdered? Who'd want to kill..." Emma stopped speaking. "Are the girls in the area?"

"The girls?" I asked.

"Those crazies who refuse to believe I'm their great-grandmother. One of them went to a community college to become a nurse."

"Aunt Emma, I'm not sure I understand."

"Connie and Carol." I'd been pacing around. I sat down before I passed out or threw up.

"My great-granddaughters are disturbed—their mother is too. At forty-three, my granddaughter, Caroline, will be lucky if she lives into her fifties like my daughter, who drank herself to death. Lettie did her best to help Caroline."

"Caroline's her grandniece, right?" I asked trying to keep all the family relations straight since I no longer had the family Bible in front of me as a reference.

"Yes. My dear, sweet sister set up a trust fund for Caroline years ago. She wanted my granddaughter to get a college education and treatment if she needed it so she wouldn't end up like her dead mother, Ann. I blame the Laughton side of the family I married into. There's not one of them that's clean and sober or sane. Not that we Morgans don't have our share of disturbed people on our side, too. Maybe it was the double-whammy of genes from both sides that pushed the next several generations deeper and deeper into depravity."

"In Aunt Lettie's family Bible, it says you divorced William Laughton not long after Lettie went back home to Montgomery."

"Yes. I should never have married him, but I was desperate to get out of Alabama. He was a problem from the get-go. While I was pregnant, and Lettie was around, he didn't bother me as much. Once Lettie left, all hell broke loose. Maybe it was pent-up anger for the year and a half he'd laid off getting drunk and hitting me because there was someone around to witness it. Who knows?"

"I'm so sorry to bring up all this."

"It's okay. I've had decades to deal with the fact I married an abusive man with a drinking problem. It's not such a strange or shameful thing anymore. The tragedy is that there still doesn't seem to be enough help for younger family members with mental health and drug problems. Caroline went through lots of therapy, rehab, and psychiatry. At this point, she's on so many drugs she's worse off than her mother was at the same age, not better. That Xanax is nasty stuff, especially when she drinks. Her kids didn't stand a chance."

"Connie and Carol, you mean, right?"

"Yes. I tried to keep them away from Lettie, but once they turned twenty-one, there wasn't much I could do. I warned Lettie not to let them get anywhere near her. She should have listened to me."

"Why didn't you want them to be around Aunt Lettie?"

"They're not right in the head—neither one of them. I don't know exactly when it started or how they came up with the notion, but Connie and Carol became convinced that Lettie was their great-grandma, not me. Maybe it was partly wishful thinking since Lettie was so much better off than me. Their gossipy cousin—your half-sister, Rose, had a hand in instigating the trouble."

"She did? How could she have done that?" As I asked the question, something my mother said years ago wormed its way into my conscious mind. "She told them Lettie went to stay with you because she was pregnant, didn't she?"

"Yes. Rose claimed that's why my daughter, Ann's, middle name was Letitia. My daughter was dead by the time the cousins cooked up this story, but poor daffy, stoned Caroline came to me asking if it was true. I told her no, but she was sure that's the real reason Lettie set up a trust fund for her."

"No good deed goes unpunished. I'm sorry. That must have been hurtful for you."

"It was, but life's hard, Lily. When you get to be as old as I am, you learn that hardship goes with the territory in the land of the living. I have happy memories from my life with my daughter when she was young. With Caroline, too. She spent lots of time with me when she was little while Ann went away for inpatient alcoholism treatment. I can't say the same for Carol and Connie. There was something off about them early on. That Connie, especially. She's a bad seed if there ever was one. Lettie chewed me out about saying such a thing. Given all the 'black sheep' talk she grew up with from the lofty Morgans and Bankheads and the old Alabama families they called friends, she disliked any implication that a person's destiny was in their blood. I suppose my conviction that it's in their DNA isn't so different."

"I'm sorry to put you through more anguish about family troubles. If it does turn out Carol or Connie had something to do with Aunt Lettie's death, I don't know what else you could have done."

"That's true. In fact, Lettie and I thought we'd put an

169

end to the nonsense after we did DNA maternity tests. That took some doing since I had to track down what's left of William Laughton to get him to give us a sample of his DNA. The tests proved, without a doubt, that I was their closest maternal relative and Bill was the same on the paternal side. Caroline and the girls all contributed samples, so, for a time, it appeared we'd put an end to their shared delusion. That's what Caroline called it when she discussed it with her shrink."

"What happened that started this up again?"

"My best guess is Eddie Callahan's what happened. Caroline said he was making the rounds trying to get family members to invest in some company he worked for. The company went belly up a while ago. He told the girls DNA tests aren't worth the paper they're written on. Caroline asked me about it, even though she'd used one soon after she divorced Harry Medford to get the deadbeat to kick in child support."

"Are you saying my stepfather's had recent contact with Carol and Connie?"

"Yes. How many no-good Eddie Callahans can there be in this world? You'd better watch it, too, Lily. Another defect in the Morgan DNA is a predisposition to fall for bums. Carol's barely an adult, and she's already headed to divorce court. Getting rid of Dale Matheson would be a hopeful sign that she's got a future ahead of her. From what Caroline's told me, her husband's as bad as Connie when it comes to leading Carol astray."

"Astray, how?"

"He's a computer software engineer—no degree, but an entrepreneur in his own eyes. Even my granddaughter didn't fall for that—Caroline says her son-in-law runs computer scams. When Carol left for California a few months ago, I hoped she'd finally come to her senses. I figured she filed for divorce and headed west to get away from him after he got arrested for stealing credit card numbers."

"I don't know how you've kept your sanity all these years. The Morgans and the Laughtons and the Callahans put a whole new spin on family dysfunction, don't they?"

"They sure do. I hope you'll have more sense than Lettie did. You're the cuckoo in the nest, Lily. Protect yourself." I searched for words. How do you reply to such a warning? At other times, in other contexts, I'm sure I would have disregarded Emma and relegated her story to the realm of family gossip. With all that had gone on the past two days, I couldn't do that.

"I'll do my best. The police are all over this. They're determined to figure out who killed Aunt Lettie and why. She was too good for her own good, wasn't she?" I didn't have the heart to add to her distress by telling her about the attempt on my life.

"I'm afraid so. Pretty damn fearless, too, which is also a mixed blessing. I'm glad you called, and we had this talk. It's worth it if it means you'll do everything the police ask you to do to stay safe while they catch Lettie's killer— even if it's family. Stay away from those girls. Now that Lettie's dead, they're probably swarming like a stirred-up nest of hornets trying to get their hands on her estate. Particularly if Eddie's pushing the idea they're Lettie's legitimate heirs."

"I appreciate your candidness. Aunt Lettie left an

amazing tea set for you—it's an antique with quite a history. I've got it ready to send to you."

"That would be lovely. Thank you. I wish I could travel to attend her funeral, but I'm not allowed to venture far from Willoughby Arms these days. I'll be there with you and my sister in spirit. You turned her life around, Lily. Mine, too, in a way. We were both close to hopeless, and very discouraged about the possibility of filial affection. Lettie called me so many times telling me about something wonderful you'd done for her. Bless you, for that. Bye, Lily."

"Bye, Aunt Emma."

I sat in stunned silence trying to understand what this meant for the situation I was in, and for the investigation into Lettie's murder. I needed to talk to Austin. I hoped he was still across the road at the winery or could pull off the road somewhere if he was already en route to San Jose.

I picked up my phone to call Austin. That's when I noticed I had a missed call. Someone had left a message. I recognized the number immediately. It was Judy.

"Shoot!" I'd forgotten to tell her I'd changed the gate code. It had only been a couple of minutes since her last call. I hoped she was sitting down there at the gate waiting for me. I called, but Judy didn't answer. When I listened to the message she left, my blood ran cold after the conversation I'd just had with Emma.

17

A Family Affair

"Pick up, pick up!" I said as I called Judy again. Nothing. I was about to call her a third time when Austin called me.

"Hello, beautiful, I've got good news for you. We found the name of the man who hosts and manages the Calla Lily Vineyards and Winery website."

"Dale Matheson, right?"

"Yes. How did you know?"

"I got his name from Emma Morgan—Lettie's sister. Carol Matheson is Emma's great-granddaughter and Dale, the loser Carol married, was arrested recently for phishing or some scam like that. So much for corporate intrigue, huh? This mess I'm in appears to be a family affair."

"Whoa, give me a chance to make sure I've got this straight. We made the connection right away between Carol and Dale Matheson. She filed a domestic abuse complaint against him last year. It's one of a dozen charges he's accumulated while launching his career in cyber-crime. Are you saying she's a relative?"

"I'm afraid so. Carol is Aunt Lettie's great-grandniece

and my cousin. Emma said she thought Carol was in the process of getting a divorce from Dale. Did she file a restraining order against him?"

"No. Maybe all has been forgiven, and he's joined her here in California. He's wanted by authorities up and down the East Coast. His latest scam was what got him noticed by the feds, and they've charged him with wire fraud. We're after him now, too. Not only is he a fugitive, but we can link him to the account that wired money to the hitman sent after you."

"I've got more to tell you given he's only one of my relatives I hope you'll get off the streets soon. Not even the scariest one, either. Hang on a second will you while I check to see if Judy's returned my call. Then I'll explain."

"Judy's still not there yet?"

"Nope. I'll be right back." I put Austin on hold. I hadn't heard a beep or a whoosh, but I wanted to make sure I hadn't missed a call or text.

"I'm back. There's nothing. Have you heard anything from her today?"

"No. Should I have had a call from her?"

"I don't know. She called me several times while I was on the phone with Emma, and she finally left a message saying she knows who killed Aunt Lettie, how she did it, and we can't let her get away with it. I didn't like the tone in her voice. Her message worries me too—especially that last part about not letting her get away with it. Do you think I should go check on her?"

"No! Let me call Dahlia and have her send someone to Judy's house. Don't hang up. I need to hear the rest of what you've got to tell me about the Fall of the House of Morgan."

"And Laughton and Callahan," I added.

"Okay. I'm putting you on hold," Austin said.

I called Judy again while I waited. I let her phone ring and ring, but she didn't answer. After six or eight rings, her voicemail finally came on.

"Judy, it's Lily. I'm worried about you. Call me and let me know you're okay." When I hung up, minutes passed like hours while I waited for Austin to return.

"Any luck?" I asked when our call resumed.

"Dahlia's got uniformed officers on their way to Judy's house."

"What if she's gone to confront Carol?

"Why would she do that?"

"I don't know. She's grieving the loss of her best friend. Maybe she's not thinking too clearly. If she's concluded Carol Matheson did it, what if Judy took Dr. Devers' comments about the use of a sedative to mean it was an act of mercy on the killer's part? What Dr. Devers said made it sound as if the killer still had a conscience when they killed Aunt Lettie. I wouldn't put it past Judy to believe she can talk Carol into turning herself in. Judy's too much like Aunt Lettie—always hoping there's a shred of good in troubled people—like Jesse and me."

"If she shows up at Carol Matheson's apartment, we'll know it, Lily. We've got the nurse's place under surveillance. Dahlia wants to interview the nurse about Lettie's death and the drugs found in her system, even though she's got an alibi. We're also hoping to spot Carol Matheson's husband if he shows up there. We know he's in the area, we're just not sure where."

"Thank goodness! After hearing what Emma had to

say, I'm completely creeped out. If Emma's right, it's not Carol, but the other sweet young thing in the clan who wins the biggest family psychopath award."

"Are you talking about Connie Laughton?"

"Yes. If I have anything to say about it, nurse Carol gets to go to prison for killing my aunt since she's the one with the expertise to have administered the digoxin. Much to my amazement, Connie Laughton is Carol's sister. Emma swears Connie's the scary one—the dominant psychopath, dragging her weaker sister into the muck and mire. If Connie knew enough to wield the needle that killed Aunt Lettie, I doubt she would have knocked my aunt out with a sedative first."

"Okay, so if it turns out Alexander Davidson was sedated before he was drowned, Carol must have had a hand in his murder, too."

"Especially if more chloral hydrate was used. Still, we're back to where we were a few minutes ago. Drowning him upside down in his own wine has the ring of a psychopath to it, but Connie's no more capable than Carol of doing it alone."

"Dale Matheson could have helped his wife and/or her sister hoist Davidson into the barrel, but why?"

"I don't know how it ties into Franklin's death or what Alexander Davidson's role was, but Emma told me a story that explains Aunt Lettie's murder and the attempt on my life. It's a doozy that wouldn't make it into a Hollywood script given how farfetched it is. Truth is stranger than fiction, though, isn't it?" I took a deep breath and then launched into the tale about the sisters' shared delusion that they're Lettie's great-granddaughters, despite the efforts my aunts, Lettie and Emma, made to set them straight.

"Given how confused and unstable Carol and Connie are, I could imagine they felt rage or betrayal at Aunt Lettie's refusal to acknowledge what they regard as their true relationship to her. Maybe Franklin got into the middle of it, and they decided he had to go, too."

"If Emma's right and they believe you're the cuckoo in the nest who's pushed them aside, it's no wonder they tried to have you killed. I'm not sure where they came up with the money they needed to do that, but maybe Alexander Davidson funded their scheme to get rid of you and Lettie."

"That didn't work out as planned. If they're in cleanup and getaway mode, maybe they had to shut him up. Why would they have had a bottle of the fake Calla Lily wine with them?"

"They could be running that scheme, too. Maybe they lured Davidson out there by wanting to give him an update about their progress. Or Davidson was pushing the bad wine to market, and they found out about it and threatened to use it against him. Who knows how many angles your family members are working?" Austin asked.

"Catch up with Eddie Callahan, and I'll bet he starts shoving other family members under the bus to save his neck. When he gets through with them, it won't matter that they have airtight alibis. Heck, with a little makeup, maybe my sister Rose got pulled in to sit on the patio while Connie slipped away and killed Franklin Everett. Dianne Hardy said Connie didn't look right—maybe that's because it was Rose masquerading as her cousin. Or Rose could have slipped in and taken Connie's place after she was sitting on the patio."

"I'm sure you're on to something, Lily. Who needs cousin Rose when Carol and Connie have each other? How similar in appearance are the two women?"

"I'm not sure. I don't know anyone around here who's ever seen them both, do you?"

"No," Austin replied.

"They've got to be close in age, though, since their mother, Caroline Laughton, wasn't involved with their father very long. Emma says there's no doubt Harry Medford's their daddy since Caroline had to have a paternity test done to get him to pay child support. Where are you, Austin?"

"I'm still here at the winery. Once the office manager came up with a contract with Dale Matheson's name on it, I called Rikki. Alexander Davidson signed off on the contract. Since he's dead, picking up Dale Matheson is the best chance to find out who paid to have you killed, and why. Rikki's going to visit the two shooters on her own so I can stay here. She'll bring up Matheson's name, and see if that makes either man feel more like talking."

"Will she tell them someone murdered Alexander Davidson?"

"If she thinks it'll get the conversation started or moving in a different direction, maybe. The local guy who imagined he has what it takes to become a hired killer might change his tune as the noose tightens. She's going to bring up the amount of money wired to the hitman and see if that gets a rise out of the local wannabe killer for hire. I'll bet his share wasn't half of the amount wired to the pro."

"Do I want to know how much it took to inspire two men to attempt to shoot me?"

"Fifteen thousand dollars was wired to Aldon Kutchner. That might have been only half of the payment he expected to receive, but it's still not much to end a life, is it?"

"No, it's not. I guess life's cheap to some people. That sure puts their murderous intentions into perspective when you consider what the little monsters, Carol and Connie, had hoped to gain as Aunt Lettie's heirs."

"They'd never see a penny. Your delusional cousins may not believe in DNA results, but the courts do."

"I can't wait to hear how Eddie Callahan or Dale Matheson planned to get around that bit of a bump in the road," I said.

"I'll ask them if I can get my hands on either one of them. If I had to guess, I'd bet they were trying to hustle Franklin Everett with a fraudulent Will or Codicil. If he had any written evidence to prove that's what they tried to do, it would be a reason to confront him and get him to turn it over once you showed up for the reading of the Will. When Franklin refused to say where it was, he was murdered, and his office was trashed."

"Eddie Callahan appeared to be shocked when he heard Franklin's estimate of the value of Aunt Lettie's estate. I bet he wished he'd told Connie Laughton to make a play for a bigger chunk of cash or a share of the business. Maybe she went back to try again, killed Franklin when he refused, and then tried to retrieve any written request she'd made from his files."

"You know, Alexander Davidson might have endorsed

that idea if he thought he had a better chance of controlling Connie Laughton than you."

"That seems sick enough to be true," I said, sighing. "The sad thing is, if they'd come to me, I might have fallen for the idea that Aunt Lettie had made bequests to her great-grandnieces that hadn't been written into her Will."

"Yeah, well only if your aunt had really died from natural causes. Even if Judy hadn't asked for an autopsy, you would have once Judy shared her concerns with you."

"True. If Aunt Lettie had left them an inheritance, I doubt they would have been willing to wait for her to die. In fact, if Emma's warning got through to Aunt Lettie, that could explain why she didn't leave them anything."

"You have to factor in Eddie Callahan, too. According to Dahlia, he's on the verge of bankruptcy so he could use an influx of cash in a hurry. Maybe your Aunt Emma was right, and he instigated this nightmare."

"Please tell me that horrible man is on a plane home to Alabama, and you'll have the police there to greet him when he deplanes."

"Your mother and siblings, yes. Eddie, no. Dahlia has already arranged to have someone do exactly what you suggest in terms of a welcoming party at the airport. Dahlia's also issued a call to find Eddie, Carol, Connie, and Dale. The rental car, too. Barb Benchley's hot on the trail. Dahlia says she's determined to bring them in. Anyway, Rikki and I decided I should stick around here in case Dale Matheson turns up. If that happens, I'm going to sit in on the interview with him. Right now, I'm waiting for the evidence specialists to finish their work in case they come up with something that helps identify Davidson's killer or killers." My phone rang.

"Let me pick up this call, Austin," I said without waiting for him to reply.

"Hello."

"Lily, it's me. You changed the gate code, didn't you?" Judy asked.

"Thank goodness, it's you! I'll open the gate and let you in. When you get here, I'll give you the new code. I've got Austin on the other line. I'll get him to call off the rescue squad I asked him to send to your house when I couldn't reach you and panicked."

"There's no need to hurry," she said. I wasn't quite sure what she meant by that. "I'm heading through the gate now. I'll see you in a couple of minutes."

"Okay, bye."

"Austin, Judy's here—maybe not all here. She's clearly not on top of her game." When I told Austin what she'd said, he seemed puzzled, too.

"I'll call you if I get any news for you. You seem to be ahead of the curve when it comes to keeping up with the latest developments, though."

"I'm trying to impress the new lawman in my life."

"It's working," Austin said as he ended our call.

By the time I got downstairs, the doorbell rang. Marlowe who must have been worn out by the events of the past few days had finally roused himself. He barked wildly when I got to the door.

"Judy, I'm so glad you're here! Marlowe's as excited to see you as I am!" I hollered as I swung the door wide open, prepared to give Judy the biggest hug of her life before lecturing her about scaring the daylights out of me. That was a mistake.

18

Blood Ties

EDDIE CALLAHAN WAS standing next to Judy. He didn't look well. Apparently, someone had decided to rearrange his face a little. Three more people stood behind him. I'd never seen the man with them before and thought he had to be Dale Matheson. He was glancing around anxiously. I wasn't sure if he was worried that they might be seen or concerned that he and the jerks with him were about to walk into a trap. I wish I'd known they were coming. I would gladly have set up a welcoming committee for them.

"We need a place to stay. Some idiot sent the cops snooping around at Judy's. You look like a perfect idiot to me, Cousin Lily." That was sweet young thing one who stood next to sweet young thing two. They weren't just sisters, but twins.

I knew I was staring at Aunt Lettie and Franklin's murderers. It wouldn't have taken them any effort at all to provide their alibis by stepping in for each other while they carried out their murderous chores. They were almost identical. One was thinner and paler than the other was, but that might not be noticeable unless they stood next to each other as they did now. The biggest difference was that the one who spoke had a demented look in her eyes to match the creepy smile on her face. That had to be Connie Laughton. Carol Matheson didn't even make eye contact with me.

"I should have put up a no vacancy sign. The Calla Lily B&B is not open for business." Before anyone could say another word or do anything, I grabbed Judy by the arm and yanked her toward me pulling her into the foyer. At the same time, I spun around and landed a well-placed elbow in Eddie's face that sent him reeling into the row of family members behind him. They were careening backward as I slammed the door and locked it. I heard screaming and what sounded like someone tumbling down the porch steps. More than one someone, if we were lucky.

"Where did you learn to do that?" Judy asked as I motioned for her to help me shove a heavy side table from the foyer in front of the door as Austin had done with the sofa at the resort's cottage. I heard a howl of rage from outside on the porch. Marlowe barked wildly in response. He ran up the stairs, and then down again.

"Andra had to get out of a tight spot more than once. Call 911!"

"They've got my phone, Lily." I looked around trying to find mine. I'd set it down when I unlocked the door. It must have fallen in my scuffle with Eddie, or when we moved that sidebar. I anxiously searched for it.

Then someone broke the window with the butt of a gun. A man's hand reached inside and grasped the doorknob groping for the lock. I picked up a shard of glass and stabbed his hand with it. He yowled as he pulled his hand back. That provoked another shriek of deranged anger from Cousin Connie.

"You've done it, now, Calla Lily. Shoot the damn lock off, Dale!" Connie demanded. With their hope of shelter gone, I felt certain they had only one other agenda at this point—revenge and the satisfaction of killing me, and most likely Judy, too. No way was that going to happen without a fight.

"Get him off me," Carol whined. "I can't move him. He's crushing me!"

"Shut up, Carol! Eddie, if you don't get up, I'm going to shoot you!" I spotted my phone, and dove for it where it had landed on the floor. As I did that, a bullet blasted the door, and the knob hung loose. Wood chips flew into my hair. When Connie gave the door a shove, it barely moved. I called 911.

"What is the nature of your emergency?" a dispatcher asked.

"Armed intruders at my home." I gave the woman my name and address, as Judy and I stepped out of the foyer and into the hallway. I kept watching the door as I waited for the dispatcher to come back on the line. It seemed to be an eternity.

"Help is on its way," the woman said. "Do you have a place to go to stay safe?"

"I've barricaded the door, but I can't tell how long that'll keep them out."

"Is there a room where you can go and lock the door?"

"Yes, if we have to do that, we will. Please, tell the police to hurry."

Connie's face moved in a tentative way as she peered in through the windows on either side of the door. The sheer fabric helped to muddle the view into the foyer, but not completely.

"They've blocked the door!" Connie bellowed. "This stupid gun isn't going to get us in there."

"Rifle in the truck," I heard a man's voice say.

"Thanks, Eddie!" Connie said, and then she must have kicked or punched him because my dirtbag stepfather cried out in pain. "Why didn't you tell us that in the first place?"

"There's another way in." I heard Carol say in a squeaky voice.

"Show me!" Connie demanded. I heard their feet pounding as they ran down the porch steps. I called Austin as Judy and I ran for the kitchen to barricade the back door.

When we got there, I dropped and shut the blinds on the kitchen windows. While I waited for Austin to answer my call, Judy and I leaned against the large rustic wooden dining table and shoved it in front of the door. It was heavy but not as hefty as the sidebar blockading the front door. Austin's cellphone was still ringing.

"Let's stack the benches on it...Austin," I said as I heard noise on the other end. "Damn! It's his voicemail."

"Austin, help! They're here! The family has arrived. They've got a handgun and Judy's rifle." Then, I texted the same message and slipped my phone into a pocket. Judy and I loaded the benches that went with the table on top of it. I wasn't sure how much good any of this would do against a loaded rifle. Then I shoved barstools from the kitchen island in front of the door, too. I dashed to the cupboards.

"Oil—where's the olive oil?" I found a large bottle and emptied it all over the kitchen floor. "That might slow them down."

"It should. Where are they?" Judy asked. "I don't hear them, do you?"

"No. Maybe they can't find your rifle. Is it in the gun rack in the cab?"

"Yes. They have the keys."

So, where were they? There should have been irate women yelling at Dale or urging each other on as they ran onto the back deck. I peeked through the blinds.

Then I heard a noise. Not outside, but in the cellar. Someone bumped into a box or a shelf—I heard a jar fall to the floor and break. A scary sound followed. It wasn't the screams of a banshee or rageful smashing of glass, but giggling. And not just coming from one of my homicidal cousins, but both. Time to go. I sent Austin another text:

My favorite spot

I pressed a finger to my lips and motioned for Judy to follow me. Then I ran back to the front door with Judy and Marlowe on my heels. When we reached the foyer, I moved the curtains to see that the porch was empty except for Eddie lying there in a heap. Either he was out cold or dead. As we shoved the sidebar out of the way, I grabbed Marlowe and uttered one word to Judy.

"Vineyards." I heard a gunshot coming from the cellar. An eerie childlike voice was next.

"Lily, come out, come out wherever you are!" Giggles

followed. Then, wailing, a thud, and the clatter of what I hoped was the rifle hitting the floor.

Judy and I were out on the porch in no time. Before we ran for it, I shut the door, hoping they might not notice immediately that we'd left that way. In a flash, we were down the steps. With Marlowe racing along with us, we crossed the driveway and ran onto the lawn that bordered the access road along the vineyards. As we reached the gravel road, I heard a shriek. A rifle blast followed even though we were clearly out of range.

"Don't stop!" I shouted and pulled Judy along with me as I plunged into the cover of the vineyards. Zigzagging our way through the rows, I yelled even though I was nearly breathless.

"If no one had heard the rifle blast in the kitchen or the gunshot at the front door, they must have heard that one," I cried. Judy didn't respond. When I turned around, she was bent over as if in pain.

"Sorry, Lily, keep going. I'm getting too old for this crap."

"Is it your heart?" I asked.

"No. Can't...get...my...breath!"

"Okay. Take it easy. I searched around for a place within the rows of vines that hadn't been thinned yet and that might hide us. There was more shouting now. Not just behind us, but down below us. Sirens were wailing, too, but still off in the distance. Another rifle blast rang out. The shooter was closer now, but this time someone returned fire.

Judy was down on her knees. She didn't respond when I tried to get her to stand. I put both arms under hers and dragged her into the place nearby that offered the best cover I could find.

"Come, Marlowe!" I commanded. He obeyed instantly and crawled into the hollow in which we hid. He crouched down close to Judy as if keeping watch over her. I prayed whoever was returning the gunfire would find us before my poor excuse for a crime family headed by two rejects from a diabolical girl band could get lucky. Or before they succeeded in killing another person who meant more to me than anyone other than Aunt Lettie. Judy's breath was shallow, and she was cold and clammy. The sirens were loud now. The police had to be at the gate.

"Hang on, Judy. Marlowe, stay! I'm going to get help." I scooted on my knees and peered through the vines looking for feet or motion. Then, I stood and ran down the slope. I didn't get far before I heard footsteps behind me. A gun cocked. A shot fired.

I heard a grunt as someone hit the ground. I turned to see Connie Laughton lying in the dirt. The gun she'd dropped was just beyond her reach. As her fingers stretched out to retrieve it, Austin spoke.

"Touch it, and you're dead." I felt like begging him to shoot her quick. I wasn't convinced she cared enough about her life for his threat to stop her. Blood poured from her a knee where Austin must have shot her and sent her toppling to the ground. Either the pain from her wound, or some lingering desire to live, caused her to stop moving, and lie there motionless. Austin shook his head as he gazed at me.

"This isn't your favorite spot," Austin said, and then gave out a loud whistle. "Here! We're over here." A stampede was on its way if the commotion descending upon us was any indication. Austin motioned for me to come to him. I ran back up the slope past creepy Cousin Connie and clung to Austin as he embraced me. "Are you hurt?"

"I don't think so." I had blood on me, but I didn't think it was mine. "We need to help Judy!" I searched to find the spot where Judy was hidden. As Jesse came running down to us, I dove into the vines nearby. "Help Judy, please!" Together, Jesse and I pulled Judy out into the open.

"Help me do what?" she mumbled. She struggled to sit up. I was so overcome by relief that I collapsed next to her laughing and crying at the same time. Dahlia dashed toward us with an EMT carrying an emergency kit. Behind him, another EMT and what looked like a member of Jesse's crew followed with a stretcher. When Judy struggled to stand, the EMT restrained her.

"Oh, stop it!" she said. "I'm okay! I'm just not used to running an obstacle course with Lara Croft Tomb Raider here." I laughed again, giddy with relief that she was feisty and able to joke about running for our lives.

"Let them check you out, Judy. Please! Someone's got to help me clean up all that olive oil."

"That isn't going to be the only mess to clean up," Judy said, shaking her head. Then she smiled at the nice looking EMT kneeling beside her. He'd opened the kit and pulled out a stethoscope. "Okay, honey, do your thing."

19

The Cleanup

"WHERE'S EDDIE CALLAHAN and Connie's vile twin sister?" I asked Dahlia after I gave the little crowd of people standing around us a quick rundown of events that had sent us fleeing into the vineyards. My voice had broken when I told them about the deranged giggles that had convinced me Carol was as far gone as her sister. That memory might haunt me longer than dodging bullets for the second time.

"You can take it easy now, Lily. We've rounded up all of them. Dale Matheson isn't in great shape and blames you for that. He says you stabbed him."

"Self-defense," I snapped.

"Your stepfather's not doing well either."

"I didn't do it," I added defiantly. "I almost wish I had! The dirty rat had it coming to him."

"Getting what's coming to him isn't over yet—in the legal sense, anyway. Benchley tells me Eddie Callahan babbled on and on as they carried him by stretcher to the ambulance. He thanked them for rescuing him, claims he was being held hostage, and feels lucky to be alive.

According to Eddie, he's an innocent victim not a dirty rat." I rolled my eyes at that. "Yeah, I've heard it all before. We'll have a nice long chat once they check him out in the ER and the doctor gives us the green light to interview him."

"I can probably tell you almost anything you want to know," Judy said, as the EMT put his stethoscope away. He'd listened to her heart, taken her pulse, and had done a few other quick checks. Then he had her move each limb, and flex her hands and toes.

"Her vital signs are good. Nothing seems broken. No obvious injuries. Can I help you get up on your feet, Judy?" When she nodded, he offered her his hand. I held out mine to her, too, and a few seconds later, she was standing. She brushed the dirt from her pants and pulled a twig out of her hair. Then she began to tell us what had happened to her before she arrived on my doorstep.

"I opened the door to let Carol into my house. After Marcia Devers called me this morning, I knew Carol did it. I remembered a conversation I'd had with Lettie about being glad she could help a relative who was struggling to restart her life. For some reason, I didn't make the connection to Carol Matheson when Lettie told me that. It wasn't until we heard Connie Laughton's name, and you asked me about it, Lily, that I went back over Lettie's stories about her screwy family ties. This morning, I remembered a problem Lettie mentioned five or six years ago about the newest generation of Laughtons. That's when I recalled she'd mentioned her sister's granddaughters—'troubled girls' as in more than one, and sisters. It was suddenly clear as a bell that they'd given each other an alibi." When Judy paused, I thought maybe she was feeling short of breath again.

"Are you okay? Do you want to sit down for a second?"

"I'm fine, physically. It's just a shame your aunt and I are such old fools. When I called and left a message for you, I told you I knew who did it. I don't know why I didn't call the police! When she turned up at my door, I hoped Carol was there to confess and wanted me to go with her to turn herself in. Then her pals barged in with a gun looking for a place to hide. They locked me in the bathroom, but I could hear them—especially when it got heated. My guess is that the fighting started before they arrived. As soon as I was out of the way, Dale and Connie demanded that Eddie give them some of the money he got from Franklin Everett so they could escape. When Eddie claimed he didn't have it and couldn't get it because his wife took the checks with her, they worked him over."

"How long were they there?"

"Not long, maybe twenty or thirty minutes. It seemed like an eternity as they grew more frantic. I knew someone was going to get hurt." Judy gulped. "The longer I listened to their sickening conversation, the more scared I became that they'd rob me and then kill me." Austin nodded.

"I can understand that as desperate as they sounded about money."

"Well, whatever they were planning, it all changed when Dale spotted a police car."

"Yeah, we sent someone to check on you after Lily told Austin you hadn't arrived yet and that she'd picked up an odd message from you. After they saw you leave, the officers drove around back to turn around and found the rental car," Dahlia offered.

"Thank goodness Barb came looking for me but didn't try to pull me over. When she pulled into the driveway, my uninvited guests hustled me out the back to my truck. I had to wave at Barb as we went by, or that deranged one swore she'd shoot me," Judy said pointing at Connie who was being hoisted onto a stretcher a few yards down the slope from us. "She was crouched down in the seat with a gun poking into my ribs, so I didn't argue with her."

The EMT tending to Connie had staunched the flow of blood and bandaged her knee. Maybe she'd knocked out Connie since my cousin hadn't uttered a sound. Maybe she was afraid Austin was still close enough to make good on his threat to shoot her.

"Are you able to walk back to the house so I can get you water or something else to drink?" I asked. "You can sit down, and tell us the rest of the story."

"I already told you I'm fine. Ask the big guy who's handy with a stethoscope, he agrees with me. Right?" The EMT who'd assisted her had packed up his kit and was prepared to leave. When Judy asked that question, he nodded and smiled.

"Lara Croft Tomb Raider's got nothing on you! Unless she tells you otherwise, I'd take her at her word. Clear liquids and a comfortable chair sound good to me."

"Will that be okay with you, Dahlia?" I asked. "We'll find a place to sit that's not in the way of the investigators."

"Sure. There's no dead body in there, just broken glass and debris from the gun blasts. They're taking pictures, and picking up fingerprints from the doors and knobs. Your olive oil trick caused one of the evidence specialists to have a little mishap." Dahlia smiled. "We'll all have to watch our step."

"I can help my two favorite women do that, starting right now," Austin said as he slid one arm around Judy's waist and the other around mine. "You don't mind, do you?"

"I don't mind a bit. I bet Lily doesn't either."

"How did they get into the cellar?" Austin asked as we walked slowly out of the vineyard toward the gravel road. "Lily and I checked and didn't see a way in or out other than the stairs in the kitchen."

"Lettie was worried that once she turned the place into a B&B, a guest would get locked in down there, so she put in a door under the stairs that leads out back. I'm not sure how Carol found it. It would have been just like Lettie to give Carol the run of the house while she was visiting—especially if Lettie had picked her out as another family member to be rescued."

"I'm sure you're right," I said. "I switched out the gate code this morning worried that Aunt Lettie might have given the old one to Carol. Lettie's sister, Emma, told me my aunt wouldn't listen even though she'd tried to explain how seriously disturbed they'd become. What I don't get is why, if Carol had the code, whoever tried to get in here yesterday stopped and spoke to Jesse rather than just coming in through the gate."

"Neither one of them can think straight, Lily. That's got to be clear to you by now." I nodded in agreement with Judy since whatever they were up to had to be rooted in delusion. Austin offered another explanation for the behavior.

"Maybe Connie or Carol—whichever one was driving—planned to do that, except that your old boyfriend was playing security guard down there. When Peter March gets here, we'll have him tell us how to find and reinforce all the weak spots on the property."

"I take it Peter March is the security consultant you contacted."

"Yes. He can inspect the property, and we can ask him to come back tomorrow if the evidence specialists aren't done in the house and cellar," Austin offered. I nodded as I pulled my cellphone out of my pocket and checked the time. So much had gone on this morning, it was impossible to believe that it wasn't even noon yet.

"There's no time like the present," I mumbled. "We're not just talking about weak spots, but gaping holes like in the hull of a sinking ship. Bring on the security consultant!" Even though I was relieved at what finally felt like the end to the relentless barrage of shocks, I was taking no chances. I'd sleep a whole lot better if we mended the hull to keep the ship afloat. Resting easy also meant making sure I understood all that had happened and why.

"How did Alexander Davidson get mixed up with my criminally insane family members?"

"Carol blamed Eddie," Judy responded. "She wailed at him wishing she'd never told him Davidson was giving 'Great-grandma' a hard time. I'm not sure how that means Davidson was able to talk her into getting rid of Lettie, but she was carrying on about that, too."

"Geez, after murdering her, she still referred to her as

Great-grandma?" Dahlia asked.

"Yep—along with some sick, self-pitying statement about '*having* to kill her' and 'it was all for nothing,' now. Her whining turned into weeping at that point." Judy looked at me as I spoke to Dahlia.

"She's delusional *and* a psychopath," I groused, still hanging onto Austin as we left the cover of the vineyards. "There's DNA proof that Aunt Lettie wasn't her great-grandmother."

"Austin tried to give me a heads-up about them, but I'm lost," Dahlia said. "It's clear the two women are relatives, but not Lettie's great-granddaughters. What I don't understand is how they planned to get control of Lettie's estate given she'd left a Will naming you as her heir, Lily. When I spoke to Beth Varner this morning, I asked her if Connie Laughton made a claim to Lettie's estate by producing another Will or Codicil when she met with Franklin Everett."

"And?" I asked Dahlia, wanting to hear the punchline.

"Beth says Connie Laughton insisted on meeting with Franklin, privately, and he'd never said much except that it was a sensitive personal matter. She took that to mean the young woman was in trouble with a man—domestic abuse or something like that." I shook my head as we stepped onto the lawn approaching the house.

"I'm sure he must have discussed this with Aunt Lettie. Isn't there a paper trail that'll give us a hint of what Connie was there to do? Given that she's a suspect in his murder, she's not protected by attorney-client privilege."

"So far, nothing has been found that says a word about what Connie and Franklin were discussing. Maybe when she killed him, she removed the contents of the files that had anything to do with her. From your aunt's file, too, since there doesn't seem to be any reference to her there either."

"If she didn't get rid of it right away, the documents could still be among her belongings or at her sister's apartment, along with the digoxin and chloral hydrate Carol used," Judy said. Dahlia shrugged.

"Evidence specialists are at Carol's apartment as we speak. Let's see what they find. The cleanup is still underway at Franklin Everett's office, too. Beth may still come up with something in writing." I pawed at the ground in frustration.

"I don't want them to get away with Aunt Lettie or Franklin's murder. It's not right!" Austin pulled me a little closer.

"They won't. Connie Laughton's going to prison for a long time, no matter what. She's going to be charged with the attempt she made on your life today," he asserted. "She and her sister will both be charged with kidnapping, assault, breaking and entering, and lots of other offenses, including the murders of Lettie and Franklin. Davidson's murder, too, if we can link Connie or Carol to an earring the evidence specialists found in the storage room at the winery."

"I'll testify that Connie killed Franklin. I heard her tell Carol to shut up and stop complaining—that at least she didn't have to get blood all over her like Connie had to do to keep the crooked lawyer from telling lies about them. She blamed Davidson for not getting rid of that crook first, so it's not much of a stretch to assume she murdered Da-vidson, too. She also said, 'drowning in his own wine was too good for him,' or something like that." Dahlia stopped midway when we crossed the driveway.

"You hear that, Lily? Carol and Connie aren't going to get away with anything. The conversation Judy overheard makes it clear they had it in for both men, not just Lettie." She started moving again before I responded.

"Nothing is ever clear with those two. You need to get Eddie Callahan to spill his guts. I hope you can tie that earring to Connie. Who knows for sure which sister wore it or if there's enough DNA to tell you. I don't know how similar their profiles are. I can go over the whole sordid story about what a previous DNA test revealed about their great-grandma delusion if you want to hear it." Dahlia's expression told me she wasn't sure, but she nodded her head as we moved on.

"How about putting the details in writing along with your formal version of what went on today. That way it'll all be on record, and you won't have to keep repeating the story."

"I still believe you can get Carol to confess. If you can do that, she'll 'confess' her sister's dirty deeds, too," Judy asserted. We'd made our way back to the foot of the steps leading up to Aunt Lettie's porch. The front door was wide open.

"I'm going to need to call someone to come fix the doors, aren't I? Can I do that?"

"Once we clear out, you can do anything you want. You'll need to get an insurance adjuster out here, too. Let's go inside, see how much longer the evidence specialists need, and then you can make those calls. This place is a mess, isn't it?"

"It could have been worse," Austin said.

"You can say that again. When they didn't try to keep me from overhearing their sick, stupid conversation, I figured I was a goner. I didn't expect to walk out of that bathroom until they decided I'd make a great hostage even if you didn't take the bait and let me in the front door, Lily. Thank goodness you yanked me inside before they knew what happened!"

"That must have thrown them for a loop," Dahlia added.

"It sure ticked them off," I conceded. "Fortunately, Judy and I make a pretty good team and managed to stay a few steps ahead of them."

"Quite literally since you two barely outran Connie's bullets."

"There at the end, she'd caught up with me, that's true. Which reminds me that I have Austin to thank for saving me from being shot for the second time in a matter of days."

"Just doing my duty, ma'am." He said and linked my arm in his. "Watch your step." Judy and I worked our way around the wood fragments, shattered glass, and blood that remained on the porch.

"Whoever imagined the life of an heiress was right up there with a princess sure had it wrong—in my case, anyway." The foyer was littered with splinters of wood, shiny streaks, and dirty oily footprints—some of them marked by little tags the investigators must have set up to take snapshots. "At least I'm alive to put this place back together in the way Aunt Lettie wanted it to be."

"Not to add to your Cinderella complex, but you're

going to have your hands full cleaning up the mess at the winery, too," Dahlia commented.

"What does that mean?" I asked as we walked down the hallway to the parlor. Dahlia led the way as if she lived here.

"Careful!" she exclaimed—that looks like a slippery spot." The oily streaks and footprints continued into the kitchen where I knew they'd originated. "I'm not sure exactly. How big a mess depends on how much damage Alexander Davidson did to the winery's finances. That's assuming there's some truth to Eddie Callahan's ranting that your Finance Officer was moving money into an overseas account. Eddie also claims Davidson took advantage of two 'poor mixed up girls' by offering them money to get him out of the jam he was in at the winery."

"If by that he means he paid them to get rid of Lettie after he failed to persuade her to give up her position on the board, offering to pay them off might have worked. That way, they'd get their hand on some cash without proving they were her heirs."

"That could be true, Austin, but why not do as Davidson asked, kill her and then just take the money and run?" I asked.

"There's more to it than that. Eddie's no doubt only telling half the truth—the half he hopes will get him off the hook. In the first place, he and Dale Matheson are in this up to their eyeballs. They never would have let the girls turn down an offer of cold, hard cash, for a little thing like bumping off an old lady. That doesn't mean the money Davidson offered them was enough to keep Connie and Carol from playing out their delusional scheme, too.

The two schemes really fit together, don't they?" Judy asked. A forensic investigator was still in the kitchen when we reached the doorway. By the sound of it, others were still in the cellar, too. "I'm going to take you up on that offer to sit down with a tall glass of water. Let's go back to the reading room."

"We'll have to settle for bottled water, Judy." I grabbed a few bottles from where they sat on a shelf nearby.

"And cookies," Austin added stepping carefully as he snagged the box containing leftovers from those Judy had brought us the day before.

"None of this discussion changes my original point. Even if Eddie Callahan's only got it half-right, you need to check out how much money Davidson pilfered and how much of it is left in his offshore account, Austin." Dahlia was emphatic.

"Dale Matheson can help us do that since we've already made the connection between him, the winery, and the offshore account used to pay the hitmen hired to kill Lily. If he's smart, he'll tell us everything he knows including Davidson's involvement in wine fraud," Austin said.

"Given the company he keeps, he can't be that smart. Mitch Carlson's a different story. He's hired a lawyer, but he's already agreed to share what he knows about the bogus wine. He says he tipped off your aunt and then decided to keep it to himself when she turned up dead not long after that."

"There are several bottles of that horrid wine sitting in the kitchen. I'm not sure if you want your investigators to take them into evidence while they're here. I wouldn't be surprised if Mitch Carlson left those bottles for Aunt Lettie to find, although he didn't own up to it when she confronted him. I'd say that means he'd already decided to keep his mouth shut about what he knew before my aunt was murdered." Dahlia shrugged.

"We've still got lots of work ahead of us with multiple murders, misdeeds, and lots of not-to-tightly-wrapped dysfunctional family members." She shrugged again, and Judy picked up the conversation.

"What Dahlia and Austin haven't said, Lily, is that the 'he said-she said' stuff could go on for months. You already mentioned how slippery the twins are, despite their mental instability. Eddie Callahan doesn't have a record, but he's crud, so anything he says can be called into question. Dale Matheson does have a record." Judy paused as we stood in the parlor. Then she reached out and put a firm hand on my arm.

"My point is that you can't wait months for this to get sorted out. You're going to need Mitch and Jesse to get you through the cleanup process and keep the company moving along. Mitch had to be scared out of his wits at the prospect of confronting Davidson. You said yourself Alexander Davidson was off the deep end or about to take the dive."

"I hear you," I said, putting my arm around the stalwart woman. "I'm glad I'll have you to help me. Jesse and Mitch had better understand from the start, that I expect them to be trustworthy and direct, or they won't have a place at the vineyards or in the winery. I don't ever want to have another cleanup on my hands like this one."

"Spoken like a woman who's ready to take the bull by the horns!" Judy said.

"It beats getting gored in the behind and trampled to the ground," I said as I slumped into a chair next to the one Judy had taken. "Cookies, please!"

20

A Posse of Divas

Y OU NEVER KNOW what you can do until you've got to do it—like fending off armed intruders who take the concept of dysfunctional family to a whole new level. Or bringing order from the chaos they left behind. I flexed my "taking the bull by the horns" muscles and, with help, went to work turning a crime scene back into a home.

A few minutes after we showed up at the house, the police investigators cleared out. Before they left, I called the insurance adjuster. Perhaps hearing the fierceness in my voice, or maybe a lingering hint of hysteria, he arrived soon after the police left. Once he took pictures and wrote up his report, Austin walked him to the door while Judy and I cleaned up the kitchen. Then, energized by the progress we were making, we cleaned the floors in the hall and foyer.

In the meantime, Jesse sent Raul Ortiz, a contractor Lettie had used for the renovations, to help us. He installed a new door handle and patched the broken front window until he could match and cut the glass to fit. When he called Raul, Jesse also told him the door in the kitchen hadn't survived the shotgun blast, so he brought a new one based on the specs he already had. With Austin's assistance, Raul hung the new door in minutes.

I heated the Chili Relleno Casserole Judy had brought us the night before while we cleaned, and the repairs were being done. The room was soon filled with warmth and mouth-watering aromas that spurred us on. Judy had just pulled her casserole from the oven when Austin returned after escorting the contractor out. With him, now, was one of the biggest men I've ever seen.

Peter March had to be almost seven feet tall, with enough muscles to play a Marvel Comics Superhero without any padding. A ruggedly attractive man, he was an imposing figure as he scanned the kitchen. His presence was a little unsettling when he peered at us from his well-worn face that bore no hint of a smile. All business, apparently, he said little after Austin introduced him. He checked the door leading out behind the house, and then followed Austin down into the cellar.

"I'm glad he's on our side, aren't you?" Judy whispered.

"You can say that again. If we can get him to run through the vineyards, maybe we can start rumors that Big Foot's on the loose around here. That might keep the bad guys away from us."

"It might keep your B&B guests away, too." We shut up at the sound of the men coming up the stairs.

"Something smells so good," Austin said. "I'm starving."

"We're just getting ready to have a late lunch. Would you like to join us, Mr. March?" I asked.

"Please call me Peter. That's nice of you, but I had lunch on my way over here. I have a good friend who insisted I try a place in Napa. Their snap pea soba noodles were the best vegan food I've eaten on the road in a long time."

"You're a vegan?" Judy asked.

"Yes." The bewildered expression on Judy's face finally evoked a smile from the man. "I often get mistaken for a carnivore." The smile was barely a smile, but it revealed him to be a good-humored man.

"Peter won't eat anything that has a face or a mom," Austin added. "I'm going to take him upstairs, so he can look around. Would you please fix me a plate?"

"Of course," I said and gave Austin a peck on the cheek. "You'll have a glass of wine with us, won't you, Peter?"

"I'd enjoy that." As we ate, Peter talked to us about the options available to improve security. That included lots of high-tech gizmos, but humans too, including armed guards. Even after the past couple of days, I couldn't imagine having armed men patrolling the property—not here in the place I still hoped to call home. I sighed heavily, trying to imagine ever feeling completely happy and at peace again here.

That bubble of hope burst in a flash! A noise that had to be coming from the road leading up to the house, sent Marlowe into a frenzy. As the sound of blaring horns grew louder, we ran to the front door. We were in the foyer, inches from the door when the doorbell rang.

"Now what?" I asked as I tried to peer around Peter and Austin. "Even I can't possibly have more homicidal family members who aren't already in police custody, can I? Eddie Callahan and the twins are in no shape to pull off an escape attempt so soon. Please don't tell me those hitmen are on the loose again." Austin paused, frowned, and checked his phone in case he'd missed something and then shook his head.

I peeked through the part of the window next to the door that hadn't been replaced by wood. Two strange men stood on my doorstep. I stepped out of the way so Austin and Peter could handle the situation.

At the sound of another horn blast and squealing tires, I jumped out of my skin. Peeking out that window again, I caught a glimpse of a convertible as it sped into view and then disappeared behind a huge van that blocked my view. Jesse's truck wasn't far behind the convertible. He was honking crazily.

"Van," I said. "As in moving van. Movers!" I cried as the signage on the side of the van finally registered in my addled brain. When I reached for the doorknob, Austin stopped me.

"Not just movers," Austin replied. He was right. I heard yelling that included cursing in several languages. Then, I almost jumped for joy. It wasn't more despera-does; it was my posse. I reached past Austin and unlocked the door.

"I'd recognize that foul mouth anywhere!" I flung open the door and ran down the steps past men in moving company uniforms. The two men hurriedly stepped out of my way. They were clearly confused by what was going on.

"What is your problem?" Zelda Gomez bellowed as

her wild curls bounced. She and Jesse were in a stand-off like a scene from *High Noon* or some other old western. Then Zelda charged Jesse and spit out another round of curses in English and Spanish. Her French was darn good, too, but I cut her off.

"Jesse, it's okay!" I cried as I threw my arms around Zelda. Neither of them wore gun belts, but my timely embrace might have kept Jesse from getting a sock in the nose. "This is my friend. They are, too!"

Three other women sat in the convertible, apparently immobilized by the fracas. I ran to open the passenger side door, and Melody Skidmore cautiously stepped from the car, holding onto her teacup Yorkie, Darjeeling.

"Pardon us for being late to the party, but Zelda miscalculated how long it would take us to get here. I guess it's okay since the moving van is still here." Melody walked over next to me, and I gave her a hug. "She's cranky as you can tell."

"Hello, Marlowe. Darjeeling has missed you." Marlowe was delirious with joy as Melody spoke to him. Melody's tiny pooch was squirming to get down. All my women friends were out of the car now. They stared at Austin who beamed that dishy smile of his at them.

"Meet Deputy U.S. Marshal Austin Jennings," I said, still grinning from ear-to-ear delighted that these wonderful women had driven all the way from LA to visit me. "There's been some trouble around here today."

"Um, um, um, I'll just bet there has been," Zelda said in a purr mixed with her cougar growl. "It's a pleasure to meet you, Marshal."

Jesse who'd taken off his baseball cap was standing

there taking it all in. He apparently wasn't sure what to do and shifted awkwardly from one foot to another. When the women turned their gazes back to him, he folded his arms across his chest. His biceps bulged as my friends gawked.

"Jesse is it?" Zelda asked now speaking in a tone that could melt butter. "I'm sorry we didn't stop when you told us to. We were trying to surprise Lily." Jesse wasn't completely ready to let go of his anger even though Zelda had zeroed in on him with her flirty Puerto Rican charm. She was always a marvel to watch. Zelda, the makeup artist on the set of *Not Another Day*, had her testy side, but she oozed charm, too. She often used that talent as an "ego wrangler" to get a temperamental cast member back in line.

"Are you a cop, too?" Carrie Cramer asked. "You look a little like that other Jesse—the one Tom Selleck plays—your mustache isn't as bushy. It's still sexy though." Jesse took a deep breath as Carrie gave him her version of a Hollywood glamor girl smile.

"You're the woman who interviews the LA Angels baseball players, aren't you?" Carrie didn't have a chance to answer him before Julie Hemsley, the fourth passenger in the car and one of the writers on *Not Another Day*, interrupted the conversation.

"You mean Jesse Stone, don't you, Carrie? This Jesse is way too young. Now that he's not yelling at us, he doesn't look as sad and grumpy as Jesse Stone, either." Julie reached into the convertible and popped open the trunk. It was crammed full of luggage. Not just overnight bags, I noted. Zelda ran to take one of the bags Julie yanked free after a couple tries.

"I thought you told us you grow grapes up here, not a crop of big, fine-looking men," Zelda said, still flirting with Jesse. And that's when Peter March stepped off the porch from where he must have been quizzing the movers. My friends' mouths dropped open as Peter joined Austin and took up his crossed arm genie pose like Jesse.

"Meet my security consultant, Peter March," I said. He nodded, but otherwise stood there.

"Do you want your stuff or not?" I turned to respond to the gruff voice coming from behind me. The movers had been remarkably patient.

"Yes, yes, I do." I stammered. "Although I have no idea where I'm going to put it all."

"Is it furniture or clothes and personal things like yoga mats and hair dryers, or what?" Judy asked, taking charge.

"All of the above, Judy," I replied. "Divas, this is Judy Tucker. Judy, meet Melody, Zelda, Carrie, and Julie."

"Nice to meet you. You're another cast member in *Not Another Day*, aren't you?" Judy asked Melody.

"I was, but I'm dead now, too." Melody shrugged as if it didn't matter, but I knew otherwise.

"Murdered, like Andra?" I asked.

"No. A sudden illness contracted during my character's travels abroad." She sighed. "At least I got to wow my fans with a tragic deathbed performance." Melody put the back of her hand on her forehead, striking a dramatic pose.

"Give it a rest, Melody. The last thing Lily wants to talk about is death and dying now that her aunt has passed on." Zelda crossed herself as she said that. "We came to help you move in and say goodbye to Lettie. We'll miss her, too."

"When you say trouble, what do you mean?" Julie asked as she walked toward me rolling a bag behind her. I didn't respond, not sure where to begin, or how much to say with the movers still waiting.

"It's been a helluva day," Judy remarked. "Let's get you all comfy, so I can go home and see what the cops did to my place trying to round up the bad guys." That drew more wide-eyed looks from my friends.

"Can't you stay here with us tonight? Jesse will send someone to check on things at your place."

"I'll think about it, but I like to make sure the animals are fed and bedded down properly. Let's get your stuff unloaded while there's a lull in the commotion around here."

"I don't know what I was thinking. I got rid of so much, but I was shocked that what was left almost filled this enormous truck." As if to underscore what I was saying, one of the movers had hustled to the van and opened the back revealing my belongings crammed in there.

"Why not stash the furniture and art and stuff like that in the bonus room off the unfinished apartment over the garage?" Judy asked.

"Okay," I said. "Where is that?"

"Did you show me that?" Peter asked.

"No, we haven't had much free time here at the house. I didn't know it existed, either," Austin responded.

"Jesse, will you show the movers the way to the

apartment I'm talking about, please? Point out Lily's room to them, too, so they'll know where to take her clothes."

"Sure, then I need to get back to the fields to tend to the crew in case there's another problem. We're running behind after all the trouble today."

"If my goats can get along without me, your crew can manage for a few more minutes," Judy retorted. Jesse was totally over his altercation with my posse, although he still appeared to be a little uncomfortable with my friends practically drooling over him. Jesse's relief was palpable when he asked the movers to follow him and took off, leaving Judy to issue her next commands.

"Lily, you're going to have to call Lettie's friends who cater the winery open houses. Someone's got to feed us until we can get organized and restock the fridge and pantry."

"I haven't had a chance to shop," I added.

"We're here to help. You know we can handle shop-ping," Melody responded.

"Austin, honey, I need you to help me get some extra pillows and blankets off shelves in the linen closet upstairs. Maybe your friend, Peter, could come along, too. He can reach the top shelf without having to drag out a step-stool."

"It'll be a pleasure, ma'am." Austin offered her his arm which she took, and then gleefully squeezed his bicep. "You're never too old for an occasional squeeze, either, Lily." I laughed at the impossibly bizarre twists that had spun my head around since I'd come home.

"I hear you!" I said. "Grab your bags, divas, and fol-low me. I'll show you to your rooms."

"Will you also tell us what the hell's going on? We heard on *Entertainment Exposed* that someone shot at you at a resort last night! How can that be true with all this hunky muscle watching out for you?"

"It's true, I'm sorry to say. No more trouble tonight, though, I promise!"

Then, I caught Austin's eye as he reached the top of the stairway with Judy still hanging onto him. By the way he smiled and held my gaze, I had to concede he just might make a liar out of me. Could I really get through the rest of the day without getting into more trouble?

—The End—

Thank you for reading *Lily's Homecoming Under Fire*, Calla Lily Mystery #1. I hope you enjoyed meeting Lily, Austin, Judy, the other characters in this book. Lily, Austin, Judy, and Jesse will be back. Lily's diva posse isn't going anywhere soon, either.

What does the future hold for Lily and her friends? When they find skeletal remains while trying to get a production ready at the outdoor theater near the Calla Lily Vineyards, there's a new mystery to be solved. Stay tuned for *Buried Secrets, Tangled Vines*, Calla Lily Mystery #2.

I'd love to hear from you about *Lily's Homecoming Under Fire*. Please leave a review or contact me by email at burke.59@osu.edu.

Recipes

Sliced Sweet Potato Pie with Molasses Whipped Cream
Serves 8

Ingredients

2 9-inch pie crusts, thawed [or make your own, if you prefer]
1 1/2 pounds sweet potatoes (about 4 medium)
1 cup light brown sugar
1/2 teaspoon cinnamon
1/8 teaspoon nutmeg
1/2 teaspoon ginger
1/4 teaspoon salt
6 tablespoons butter
1/2 cup heavy cream

Preparation

Boil sweet potatoes until half cooked, 15 to 20 minutes and let them cool enough that you can handle them.

Peel and slice sweet potatoes thinly [about ¼ inch].

Mix brown sugar, cinnamon, nutmeg, ginger, and salt.

Place a layer of sweet potatoes in the bottom of a 9-inch pie pan lined with one of the pie crusts. Sprinkle the potatoes with some of the spice mixture; dot with a little bit of butter.

Continue adding layers until all ingredients are used, dotting the top layer with butter. Pour the cream over the layers.

Top the pie with the second crust, fluting the edges and then cut several vents into the top.

Bake at 425 degrees Fahrenheit for 30 for 40 minutes.

Using a toothpick, check to make sure the sweet potatoes are tender. They ought to yield easily to the toothpick. If not, reduce the temperature to 350 degrees Fahrenheit and continue baking, checking every ten minutes or so until they're done.

Molasses Whipped Cream
Makes 2 ¼ cups

Ingredients
1 cup cold whipping cream
2 Tablespoons molasses [not blackstrap]
½ teaspoon vanilla

Preparation
Using chilled beaters and a large chilled bowl, beat cream with an electric mixer on high speed until thickened, about 2 minutes.

Add molasses, and beat until stiff peaks form, another 2 minutes.

Add vanilla extract and beat 1 more minute.

Cover and chill until ready to serve.

Transparent Pie
8 servings

Ingredients

Crust
1 cup all-purpose flour
1/4 cup of granulated sugar
1 teaspoon salt
1 1/2 teaspoon water, chilled
1/2 cup plus 2 tablespoons of unsalted butter, chilled

Filling
8 tablespoons butter, softened
2 cups granulated sugar
1 cup heavy cream
4 medium eggs, beaten
2 tablespoons all-purpose flour
1 teaspoon vanilla extract

Preparation
Preheat oven to 375 degrees.

Using a food processor, pulse together flour, salt, sugar, water and butter until the dough begins to come together and appears crumbly. Remove dough from processor and knead gently, without overworking, until the dough is formed into a 1/2-inch thick disc.

Cover with plastic wrap and refrigerate for 30 minutes. After the crust has chilled, remove from the refrigerator and allow it to rest for five minutes. Then roll out the crust, press into a pie plate or pan, crimping the edges and removing any excess dough. Set aside.

With an electric mixer, beat the butter and sugar together until the mixture is smooth, about 3 minutes. Add cream and eggs and beat again until smooth. Then stir in flour and vanilla with a large spatula or spoon.

Pour filling into the crust. Bake until a golden-brown crust forms on top and a toothpick inserted comes out clean, about 45 minutes.

Sweet Alabama Pecan Bread

8-12 servings

Ingredients

1 cup sugar
1 cup brown sugar
4 eggs beaten
1 cup vegetable oil
1 1/2 cup self-rising flour
1 teaspoon vanilla
2 cups finely chopped pecans

Preparation

Preheat oven to 350 degrees.

Lightly grease and flour a 9-inch-by-13-inch baking dish.

Stir together sugar, brown sugar, eggs and oil in a bowl until the mixture is smooth.

Stir in flour and vanilla, add pecans, and stir again until all the ingredients are evenly mixed.

Spoon into prepared pan and bake for 30-35 minutes.

Chocolate Chip Cookies
About 2 Dozen Cookies

Ingredients

1 cup dark brown sugar, firmly packed
1/2 cup granulated sugar
1 cup (2 sticks) cold salted butter, softened
2 large eggs
2 teaspoons vanilla extract
2 1/2 cups all-purpose flour
1/2 teaspoon baking soda
1/4 teaspoon salt
2 cups (12 ounces) semi-sweet chocolate chips
1 cup chopped pecans [optional]

Preparation

Preheat oven to 350 degrees F.

In a large bowl, combine the butter, sugars, eggs, and vanilla.

In a separate bowl, mix together the flour, salt, and baking soda.

Combine the wet and dry ingredients.

Stir in the chocolate chips and add the chopped nuts if you're using them.

Scoop golf ball-sized dough portions and place 2 inches apart on an ungreased cookie sheet.

Bake for 9 to 10 minutes or just until the edges are light brown. They'll still be soft in the middle. **Don't overcook if you like your cookies chewy or bake a few minutes longer if you prefer them crispy.**

Easy Chili Relleno Casserole
Serves 8

Ingredients

4 eggs

1 1/2 cups milk

2 tablespoons all-purpose flour

1/2 teaspoon pepper

1/4 teaspoon salt

1/2 teaspoon paprika

1/4 teaspoon cayenne

3 7-ounce cans whole green chilies, split open

4 cups shredded cheddar (about 1 pound)

4 cups shredded Monterey Jack (about 1 pound)

1/4 cup fresh cilantro, chopped for garnish

Preparation

Preheat oven to 350°F.

Lightly grease 9x13-inch glass baking dish. Beat eggs, milk, flour, and spices to blend. Arrange chilies from 1 can in prepared dish, covering bottom completely.

Sprinkle with 1/3 of each cheese. Repeat layering twice. Pour egg mixture over the layers. Let stand 30 minutes.

Bake until casserole is slightly puffed in center and golden brown on edges, about 45 minutes. Cool 20 minutes, garnish with fresh cilantro, and serve.

Sugar Snap Pea Soba Noodles

Serves 6

Ingredients

<u>Soba</u>

6 ounces soba noodles or spaghetti noodles of choice*
2 cups frozen organic edamame
10 ounces (about 3 cups) sugar snap peas or snow peas
6 medium-sized carrots, peeled
1 red bell pepper
1/2 cup chopped fresh cilantro (about 2 handfuls)
1/2 cup toasted sesame seeds

<u>Ginger-sesame sauce</u>

1/4 cup reduced-sodium tamari or soy sauce*
2 tablespoons high quality peanut oil or extra-virgin olive
  oil
1 small lime, juiced
1 tablespoon toasted sesame oil
1 tablespoon honey or agave nectar
1 tablespoon miso of choice
2 teaspoons freshly grated ginger
1 teaspoon chili garlic sauce or sriracha

*If you choose 100% buckwheat soba noodles and gluten free soy sauce, this is not only a wonderful vegan dish, but gluten free, too!

Preparation

Slice the peas in half lengthwise or roughly chop them. Slice the carrots into long, thin strips with a julienne peeler, or slice them into ribbons with a vegetable peeler.

Remove the stem and seeds from the red bell pepper and cut it in half and then lengthwise in thin slices.

To make the sauce: whisk together the ingredients in a small bowl and set aside.

Bring two big pots of water to a boil.

In one pot, cook the soba noodles just until al dente, according to package directions (usually about 5 minutes), drain and rinse under cool water.

Cook the frozen edamame in the other pot until warmed through (4 to 6 minutes) and then drain them.

Combine the soba noodles, edamame, snap peas, bell peppers, and carrots in a large serving bowl. Pour in the dressing and toss. Add the chopped cilantro and toss again.

Serve the noodles, sprinkling them with the toasted sesame seeds.

About the Author

An award-winning, USA Today and Wall Street Journal bestselling author, I hope you'll join me *snooping into life's mysteries with fun, fiction, and food—California style!*

Life is an extravaganza! Figuring out how to hang tough and make the most of the wild ride is the challenge. On my way to Oahu, to join the rock musician and high school drop-out I had married in Tijuana, I was nabbed as a runaway. Eventually, the police let me go, but the rock band broke up.

Retired now, I'm still married to the same sweet guy and live with him near Palm Springs, California. I write the Jessica Huntington Desert Cities Mystery series set here in the Coachella Valley, the Corsario Cove Cozy Mystery Series set along California's Central Coast, The Georgie Shaw Mystery series set in the OC, The Seaview Cottages Cozy Mystery Series set on the so-called American Riviera, just north of Santa Barbara, and The Calla Lily Mystery series where the murder and mayhem take place in California's Wine Country. Won't you join me? Sign up at: http://desertcitiesmystery.com.

Made in the USA
Middletown, DE
22 June 2020